Two Cool for School

by Belle Payton

Simon Spotlight

New York London Toronto Sydney New Delhi

SIMON SPOTLIGHT
An imprint of Simon & Schuster Children's Publishing Division
1230 Avenue of the Americas, New York, New York 10020
© 2014 by Simon & Schuster, Inc. All rights reserved, including the
right of reproduction in whole or in part in any form.
SIMON SPOTLIGHT and colophon are registered trademarks
of Simon & Schuster, Inc.
Text by Sarah Albee
For information about special discounts for bulk purchases, please contact Simon &
Schuster Special Sales at 1-866-506-1949 or business@simonandschuster.com.
Manufactured in the United States of America 0414 OFF
First Edition 10 9 8 7 6 5 4 3 2 1
ISBN 978-1-4814-0644-4 (pbk)
ISBN 978-1-4814-0645-1 (hc)
ISBN 978-1-4814-0646-8 (eBook)
Library of Congress Catalog Card Number 2013946998

CHAPTER ONE

"Perfect."

Alex Sackett stared down at the pale-yellow wrap dress she'd laid out on her bed and nodded with satisfaction. Combined with her brand-new, first-ever pair of cowboy boots, it would be just the right first-day-of-school outfit. She even had a matching yellow headband to wear with it. *Whew!* Alex thought. *Talk about a down-to-the-wire decision. School starts tomorrow!*

She frowned at the heap of discarded clothes on the floor. She'd had to try on half her wardrobe before arriving at the perfect combo, so it was going to take a while to get her room back in shape. And she still had new vocabulary cards to memorize—she tried to memorize five each day.

Alex guessed that her twin sister, Ava, was not laying out her school outfit or memorizing vocab words. Ava wasn't someone you'd describe as a slave to fashion. Just last week she'd appeared at breakfast wearing one of their brother Tommy's T-shirts, inside out. Nor was Ava the plan-ahead type. Alex hoped that maybe this year she'd be able to convince Ava to try getting her stuff ready the night before, so their mornings would be less rushed. Alex loved her twin sister, but she could be pretty disorganized.

The smell of cookies wafted up the stairs, and Alex heard the oven door slam.

"Al! Tommy! Cookies!" yelled Ava from the kitchen.

With one backward glance at the outfit she'd chosen—maybe she should go with the green dress instead?—Alex headed downstairs.

"Second batch will be out in just a couple more minutes," said their dad, Mike Sackett—or Coach, as Ava and Tommy called him. He had tied on one of Mrs. Sackett's ruffled aprons, which made Alex giggle. It was a funny accessory on such a big, athletic-looking guy, complemented by the flowery oven mitts he wore to pull cookies out of the oven. Coach loved to bake, and it was a Sackett family tradition to have milk and cookies the night before the first day of school.

"Got that outfit all set, Al?" asked Ava with a mischievous grin as Alex poured herself a glass of milk. Ava was sitting at the kitchen table, with their school schedules side by side in front of her. They had gone to Ashland Middle School earlier that day to pick them up and take a tour.

"Ave, don't tease your sister," said Coach as he transferred cookies to a cooling rack. Moxy, the Sacketts' energetic Australian shepherd, sat beneath him, waiting hopefully for a cookie to fall to the floor. "It's natural to be a little nervous for your first day at a new school. New town. New state. It's a big change."

"I'm not nervous so much as apprehensive," said Alex, who liked to work her vocab words into sentences as often as possible. She sat down next to her sister to look at their schedules.

"We don't have a single class together," said Ava with a frown. "Not even homeroom."

"We have the same lunch period," Alex noticed.

"You have Mr. Kenerson, the middle school football coach, for homeroom," Ava said, pointing to the name at the top of Alex's schedule.

"Oh, great," she said, blowing back a stray curly tendril that had escaped her ponytail. "You're the one who knows football, but I get the coach. He'll probably expect me to know every play in Daddy's playbook."

"Maybe it'll inspire you to learn a little about the game," said Ava. Their dad set a platter of cookies in front of them, and she helped herself to one of the biggest ones, which was still gooey in the center. "I mean, we have just moved to a football-crazy part of Texas, and our dad is the head coach at the high school."

"Studying up on the rules is definitely on my to-do list," said Alex. "Look, you have Ms. Kerry for homeroom. She's my math teacher."

"Awesome, she'll expect me to be as brilliant as my twin sister," said Ava drily.

Just then their mother burst into the kitchen with the phone in her hand. Her eyes were shining. "Guess what? I just got my first big—and I mean big—order!"

"Aw, honey, that's terrific!" said Coach. He tugged off his oven mitts and gave her a hug.

"What's the order for, Mom?" asked Alex. Their mother was a potter, and Alex had recently helped her create a new website to sell her pieces.

"Remember Katie McCabe, Daddy's colleague back at the old school in Massachusetts? She's registering with me for her wedding!" said Mrs. Sackett. "I'll be making plates, bowls, coffee cups, serving platters—the works!"

"I knew your business would take off fast," said Alex. "You're so talented, Mom."

"Of course she's talented," said their older brother, Tommy, walking into the kitchen with his easy athletic gait. "Where do you think I get all my talents from?" He grinned and put an arm around his mother's shoulders. Alex was still not used to seeing her sixteen-year-old brother looming over their mom. He'd probably grown six inches in the past six months. He was looking more and more like their dad every day—he wasn't as bulky as Coach yet, but he was getting there.

"It's going to be a busy next few weeks, Michael," said Mrs. Sackett, helping herself to a cookie. "I was talking with April Cahill earlier today, and she casually mentioned that as the coach's wife, I'm more or less expected to plan a barbecue for the team for Homecoming weekend. And evidently your predecessor's wife gave each player a towel with his initials embroidered on it!" She shook her head and chuckled in disbelief.

Alex studied her dad's face. He laughed along with her mom, but it was an uneasy laugh.

Mrs. Sackett must have noticed this too. She raised her eyebrows. "What?" she said, laughing. "You don't seriously think I should take up embroidery, do you, hon?"

"Oh, no, no, of course not, Laur," said Coach as he put a large football-shaped cookie down in front of Tommy. "But you know as well as I do that the role of a coach's wife comes with its own set of expectations and pressures."

Mrs. Sackett sighed and took a bite of her cookie. "I know," she conceded. "It's just that it's a bigger deal here than it was in Boston," she said. "Every time I turn around, people ask me about the team, your strategies. The newspapers call practically every day. And now I've got this huge order."

"You should concentrate on building your business, Mom," said Tommy as he stood up from the table, his cookie only half-eaten. "So we can afford that piano."

"There he goes with the piano again," said Alex to Ava in a low voice.

Tommy gave his dad a playful block with his shoulder as he headed out of the kitchen. A couple of minutes later they heard the sound of his keyboard up in his room.

Their mom and dad exchanged a look.

"Something bothering Tommy?" asked Mrs. Sackett.

Coach shrugged. "I think he's a little bent out of shape that he's third-string quarterback, behind PJ Kelly and Dion Bell. But he's still growing—he's got the talent to be a really fine quarterback. He doesn't have to give up on football yet!" he joked.

"But maybe with my business starting to grow, we should consider getting that piano he's been asking about," said Mrs. Sackett thoughtfully.

Coach turned back to his tray of cookies. "It's just a phase. Football and music just don't mix."

Now it was Ava and Alex's turn to exchange a look. Alex didn't think Tommy's love of music was "just a phase."

Ava slid out of her chair. "Thanks for the snack, Coach," she said, and headed upstairs.

Ava heard Tommy playing an old-time jazz piece and quietly let herself into his room. She sat on his bed as he finished.

"That sounded great," she said. "You're really good, Tommy."

He shrugged. "It would be nice to have a real piano," he said. "But I think Coach would sooner put a gridiron in the backyard than buy one." He plunked himself down onto the bed next to her. "I did discover a really great piano—a Steinway baby grand!—at the church on the corner. And they said I can play it anytime I want as long as there isn't a service going on."

Ava loved how psyched her brother got when he talked about music. "Is there a piano at the high school, too?"

Tommy's blue eyes danced. "Yup, several. And I think they maintain them pretty well. I'm going to the info session for the concert jazz band after school tomorrow."

"How can you be in the band, with football?

Are you going to change uniforms for the half-time show?"

"It's not the marching band, goofball," he said, grinning. "It would be hard to march with a piano. But the concert jazz band is really good. Rehearsals are last period during sports study hall. That's when we're supposed to be in the trainer's, getting taped and suited up for practice. So it might mean I'm a few minutes late for practice twice a week, but whatever. I'm only the third-string QB, Ave. And this is an incredible group."

Ava swallowed down a worried lump that had risen in her throat. "Music is really important to you," she said. "You're right, you should at least go to the info session. Maybe you and Coach could work something out," she added, but her voice faltered a little. She was pretty sure Coach wouldn't care how incredible the concert band was—she wasn't sure if he would ever understand if his own son, a talented athlete, chose piano over football.

"Thanks, pal," said Tommy. "Now get out of here. I have to pick out my outfit for tomorrow."

An hour later Ava joined her sister to wash up in the small bathroom the girls shared. It wasn't quite the same as sharing a bedroom, as they'd done back at their old house in Massachusetts, and it was pretty cramped for two, but they'd learned to take turns at the sink, and the bathroom was quickly becoming the girls' favorite place to touch base and recap their days together.

"So, Ave," said Alex briskly, rinsing off her electric toothbrush and putting it back in its charger. "Do you promise me you'll get up on time? Maybe even a little earlier than usual, so our first morning isn't the usual mad rush for the bus? It's stressful enough starting a new school. I don't want to be stressed waiting for you, too."

"Yes, I promise," said Ava, running a comb through her short wavy dark-brown hair. She'd had long hair like her identical twin until very recently, when she'd gotten a dramatically shorter cut so it was easier to play sports. At first Alex had been really upset with Ava for making such a drastic change without talking to her first, but the twins had since talked about it and made up. Now Alex called Ava's haircut "adorable" so often that Ava wondered if Alex was going to cut her hair too. "I'm going to set my alarm clock and set an alarm on my phone, and I'm going to put them both across the room so I can't fall back asleep."

"Good," said Alex, but Ava could still see little lines of tension in her neck. She and Alex had always shared a near-telepathic ability to read each other's moods and feelings, and Ava could tell Alex was nervous about their first day at Ashland Middle School. Ava was too—sixth grade in Boston was still a part of elementary school, so this was the first year the twins would be switching classes. Ava sometimes had a hard time keeping track of assignments with one teacher; she wasn't sure how well she would be able to handle having six teachers. She gave herself a little shake as she rinsed off her toothbrush. It would be okay.

Alex paused at the doorway to her room and turned back toward Ava. "It's going to be a great first day of school, right, Ave?"

Ava smiled back at her. "It's going to be awesome."

CHAPTER TWO

"Gahhhh!"

Alex gave a loud cry of exasperation. She finished her eggs and slammed her fork onto her plate. Ava had overslept. Even though she'd promised Alex over and over again last night that she wouldn't. Alex had heard both of Ava's alarms blaring at 6:25 while she was in the bathroom putting the finishing touches on her hair. She had even called to Ava to be sure she was awake, and Ava had assured her that she was.

But then she hadn't appeared at breakfast, and now it was seven o'clock. The bus was due to arrive at 7:20, and they'd been told to be at the stop at least fifteen minutes early because bus routes on the first day of school were always chaotic.

"You go on," said Mrs. Sackett, thrusting Alex's lunch into her hands and propelling her toward the kitchen door. "I'll make sure Ava's right behind you."

Alex gave one last glance at her harried-looking mother. Her long wavy hair was uncombed and wild, and over her cotton pajama bottoms she wore one of Coach's old Texans T-shirts that was way too big for her. Even in this disheveled state, Alex noted, her mom still looked pretty.

"Go!" said Mrs. Sackett.

Alex went.

She didn't want to be seen running to the bus stop on her first day of school, but she set out at a brisk race-walk. Her nearly empty brand-new backpack bumped up and down with each step. The air was already warm, despite the time of day, and promised to be blazing and humid later. But Alex was getting used to the heat here in Texas. Sort of.

She rounded the corner and saw a line of four kids. She slowed her pace to a casual walk. They all turned to regard her as she said, "Good morning!" and they nodded back. Three of the kids looked like sixth graders, but one boy looked like an eighth grader. He carried what might be a French horn case and wore pressed khaki pants and leather lace-up shoes, despite the impending heat of the day.

In the distance Alex heard the *psshhh* of air brakes, and a second later the yellow school bus was visible, turning the corner at the other end of the block, heading in their direction.

Alex glanced worriedly behind her. Could it be possible that Ava was going to miss the bus on the first day of school? Her heart sank. She'd been so sure Ava was going to have her act together this morning.

Just a second or two later, Ava came careening around the opposite corner at a full sprint. Alex closed her eyes with a pained expression, and then opened them again. Ava's striped tank top was half tucked in, the hem on the right side hanging a good three inches lower than the left. In one hand she carried her partly unzipped backpack, and in the other, a half-eaten bagel with peanut butter.

Ava made it to the bus stop in a dead heat with the school bus, skidding to a stop at the end of the line just as the bus doors swished open.

The boy with the French horn took an alarmed step back as Ava bent over to catch her breath and almost dropped her bagel.

"Close call, Ave," said Alex in a low voice. "You really had me worried."

Ava stood back up and followed her sister onto the bus. "I had it all planned," she said with mock casualness, although she was clearly still out of breath from her sprint. "I just wanted to add a little bit of excitement to our first day of school."

Alex rolled her eyes as she and her sister found an empty seat toward the middle of the bus. "Ave, has anyone ever told you how exasperating you can be as a sister?"

"Yep," said Ava with a twinkle in her green eyes. "You have. Frequently."

They got to school before the first bell and were able to remember the way to their lockers, which, thankfully, were right next to each other.

"This place looks really different when it's full of kids," said Ava. She rotated her wrist to peer at the locker combination she'd written in pen on the palm of her hand. "It's about eleven times the size of our old school."

"Think of it like a big plus sign," said Alex. "There are four wings: North, South, East, and West. Remember what they told us on the tour yesterday? The gym is in the middle, and the cafeteria is on the second floor, just above it." She trailed off. "Ave? Are you even listening to what I'm saying? What? Did you forget something?"

"Um, yeah, sort of. My schedule," said Ava.

"Oh no!" moaned Alex.

The first bell rang, and the hallways swelled with kids, now moving at a faster pace to get to their homerooms.

"It's fine," said Ava. "My homeroom is right here, in the S wing. I remember that from the tour. I'm sure Ms. Kerry will be able to give me a new schedule, and besides, I think I remember every class—except when my English is."

Alex nodded and closed her locker. She moved closer to her sister and held out her fist, down low, so that Ava could bump it with her own. "Good luck," she said under her breath.

"You too. See you at lunch," said Ava, and off they went in opposite directions.

The first person Alex saw when she entered Mr. Kenerson's classroom was Lindsey Davis surrounded by a group of girls Alex didn't know. The second bell hadn't yet rung, so kids were standing around in clumps exclaiming over new haircuts, summer tans, and cute outfits.

As Alex stood near the doorway, assessing where the best tactical place to sit might be—close to the popular girls, but not so close as to suggest she thought she was already in the group—Lindsey smiled and waved her over.

Thank goodness, Alex thought. She had only met Lindsey once, but she had already figured out that Lindsey was pretty popular . . . and Alex hadn't exactly made the best first impression. Grateful for the chance to change that, she walked over and joined Lindsey's group.

"Guys, this is Alex," said Lindsey. "Alex Sackett."

Had she emphasized Alex's last name in a meaningful, nudge-nudge, do-you-know-who-this-is kind of way? Alex couldn't be sure. She wished Ava were here.

The girls all smiled and said hi, although Lindsey didn't tell Alex what their names were. To fill the awkward moment, Alex turned to Lindsey and said brightly, "I love your hair up like that!"

"Thanks," said Lindsey. "Your dress is really cute."

"Oh, thanks." Alex flicked at it casually, as though she hadn't put hours of thought into choosing her first-day-of-school outfit. "I got it at Cooper and Hunt last week."

Lindsey's smile twitched to a frown, and then became a smile again, although not quite as bright as before.

Alex wondered what she'd said wrong. Then she remembered what she'd heard about Lindsey's family. Lindsey's cousin Jack had told Ava that they were having financial troubles. Oh, great! Cooper & Hunt was kind of expensive, so now Lindsey probably thought she was spoiled and wealthy. "I got it on the clearance rack at the end-of-summer sale," she put in hastily. "It's amazing what you can get on clearance." She felt an urge to keep speaking, to smooth over the awkwardness. "I almost never buy clothes full price at Cooper and Hunt, because it's way overpriced. They have good sales, though."

Lindsey raised her eyebrows.

The bell rang, and Mr. Kenerson told everyone to take a seat.

Alex slid miserably into her chair. Was Lindsey offended? Maybe she should have just said thank you and not gone on about buying stuff on clearance. She was just trying to make Lindsey feel better!

Mr. Kenerson was taking attendance. Alex sat up straighter and paid attention to the names. The sooner she learned who was who, the sooner she could start moving forward with her plans to ascend to the top of the student government. Alex had been sixth-grade class president at her old school in Boston, and she was hoping to continue her reign here in Texas.

"Alexandra Sackett," Mr. Kenerson droned, and then his eyebrows furrowed and he looked up, startled.

"Here!" said Alex, shooting her hand up into the air.

"Are you Coach Sackett's daughter?" he asked, and the rustling of papers and snapping of binders suddenly ceased. Alex could feel the whole room go quiet, staring at her.

"Um, yes," she said. For the first time she noticed that Mr. Kenerson had Ashland Tigers pennants on his wall, and his paperweight and wastepaper basket were emblazoned with the Tigers' logo. Her stomach did a little flip. Uh-oh.

"How's the team look so far?" asked Mr. Kenerson, fixing her with a keen stare. Alex could easily conjure up a visual of him in his coaching attire, a whistle around his neck.

"Um, okay, I think," said Alex. "The first game's a week from Friday, so—"

"Does your father like the idea of his corners jamming the wideouts, or will they play off?"

Alex prayed for a miracle. Maybe the ceiling would cave in. Or the fire alarm would go off. "I don't, um, really follow—"

"Now really, Mr. K, just because her dad's the coach doesn't mean she's an expert, does it?"

Alex turned. Lindsey had saved her!

"What's that? Oh, right. Sorry. Got carried away there," said Mr. Kenerson sheepishly. He stared back down at his clipboard. "Moving along."

"And besides," Lindsey continued, "doesn't that strategy depend on how confident he is that his front four can apply pressure?"

Alex gaped at her.

"Well, I suppose that's true," mused Mr. Kenerson, stroking his chin thoughtfully. He continued with the roll call.

Alex's eyes were wide with astonishment and gratitude. "Thanks for jumping in!" she whispered to Lindsey. "I had no idea you knew so much about football!"

Lindsey smiled back at her, a hint of triumph in her expression. "No worries," she said. "You learn a thing or two when you've been cheering as long as I have."

"Oh, right," said Alex. "And cheerleading starts up soon, doesn't it?"

Lindsey shrugged. "Yeah, well, I'm still deciding if I'm even going out for the squad again," she said. She suddenly became very interested in organizing her pencil case.

Once again Alex felt baffled, like she'd said the exact wrong thing to Lindsey.

CHAPTER THREE

Ava and Alex had arranged a meeting location near the cafeteria, and Ava was glad when she spotted her sister through a gap in the throngs of kids hurrying to get in line.

"Hey," said Ava, slightly out of breath.

"Hey," said Alex. "How's it going?"

Ava hesitated. "Okay, I guess. I was late for science because I got lost. It's a really big school."

They headed toward the cafeteria together. It was easy to find—all they had to do was follow the stream of kids and the smell of pizza.

Alex nodded vigorously. "I was almost late for social studies. And people keep asking me football questions I can't answer."

"Yeah, I'm thinking of changing my last name," said Ava with a grim smile.

"Oh! Look! There's Emily and Lindsey sitting at that table over there!" said Alex, and she began waving an arm at them as though she were landing an airplane.

Ava looked. She put a restraining hand on her sister's arm, but Alex shrugged it away.

"Come on. Let's go sit with them," said Alex, and marched off in their direction.

"Al, their table already looks pretty full," Ava called after her, but she knew it was useless to try to talk her sister out of something once she had set her mind to it. She followed Alex unhappily.

"Hey, guys!" said Alex, flashing a dazzling smile.

"Alex!" said Emily, seeming genuinely pleased. "You look so cute! I love your cowboy boots!"

Ava had been hanging back, but now she stepped forward. *Maybe they will let us sit with them,* she thought.

"Mind if Ava and I squeeze in with you guys?" asked Alex, pointing to the empty space between Emily and Lindsey.

"Oh, sorry," said Lindsey, cocking her head to one side and pursing her glossy lips. "We promised Annelise and Rosa we'd save these seats for them."

"That's fine," said Ava quickly. "There are tons of empty tables still." She tried to drag Alex away.

Lindsey gestured to the lunch bags the girls were carrying. "Did you guys bring your own?" she asked. "Cafeteria pepperoni pizza not doing it for you?"

Lindsey's tone was friendly, but Ava could detect an edge to it.

Alex looked flustered. "Well, I'm a vegetarian," she admitted. "And our dad likes to make our lunches for us."

Ava spoke up quickly. "The food at our old school wasn't great," she said. "So we just got used to bringing our own."

"That's so cute that he makes your lunch," said Emily, and she seemed sincere.

"And I guess you'll get used to Texan dining eventually," said Lindsey. "There are one or two vegetarians somewhere here in the state, or so I've been told."

Ava scanned the crowd for open seats and tugged at Alex's arm a little more forcefully.

"Yo! Over here!" a voice called.

It was Jack Valdeavano, Lindsey's cousin. He

was sitting with Corey O'Sullivan and a group of other guys and girls, three tables over from Emily and Lindsey. Ava felt her heart beat a little quicker. It wasn't as though she *like* liked Jack or anything, but she definitely liked him. They'd met the first week she'd arrived, at a park in their neighborhood, and had hung out and played basketball a few times since. And he did have a pretty great smile.

"Let's go, Al," said Ava, and she pulled her sister over to where Jack and Corey were sitting.

Alex hissed into her ear. "Ave! I can't sit with Corey! Remember what you told me? I think Lindsey likes him! This could be a very bad tactical maneuver, socially speaking."

Ava had to admit she was right. Alex liked Corey, but they had recently found out that he and Lindsey used to date, so it probably wasn't the best idea to sit with him. It was too late, though—they were at the table, and Ava slid into the seat across from Jack. Alex sat down warily across from Corey. Both girls glanced in Lindsey's direction. Ava saw a dark expression pass Lindsey's face, which was quickly replaced by a smile. Ava darted a look at Alex, who had seen the same thing. Alex gave a nervous little shrug. There was nothing she could do now.

Ava unzipped her lunch and grinned at the contents. Coach had packed her a peanut butter and banana sandwich with the crusts cut off. She was way too old to be eating a sandwich with the crusts cut off—that was something pre-schoolers demanded—but her dad knew how much she hated crusts, and it was a sweet gesture for her first day at her new school. Plus, he'd packed her a football-shaped cookie.

Corey leaned forward and grinned at Alex. "I can't believe we haven't had any classes together yet," he said. "What do you have next?"

"What? Um, I think English, with Ms. Torres?" Alex's face was scarlet. She'd put her sandwich on the table but hadn't taken a single bite. "And then math, with Ms. Kerry."

"Oh, awesome—me too! So we're in two classes together. I heard Ms. Torres is tough."

"Really?" said Alex. "Well, I've already read the first book on the list, *Johnny Tremain*. Like, twice. So hopefully that will help me. Actually, I've already read most of the books on the syllabus."

"You already looked up the books on the syllabus?"

Alex laughed awkwardly. "I just wanted to

see what they read last year. You know, to prepare," she said.

Corey nodded. Ava cringed inwardly. Why
did Alex become so nervous and weird around
guys she liked?

"So who do you have for English?" Jack asked
Ava.

"Oh! I don't know. I forgot my schedule at
home and my homeroom teacher didn't have
the right printout. I have time to stop by the
office to check—actually, I should probably go
do that." She finished her sandwich hastily.

"I hope it's Palmer, next period," said Jack. "I
hear it's a pretty cool class."

Ava popped her last carrot stick into her
mouth and grabbed her cookie and apple for the
road. Then she stood up, waved to the table, and
headed for the office, trying not to feel guilty for
leaving Alex there alone.

There was already a line of kids in front of
the secretary's desk when Ava arrived. *Good,
other kids also forgot or lost their schedules,* Ava
thought, relieved. Mrs. Gusman, the secretary,
hustled the line along, looking information up
on her computer and then directing the students
where to go.

"Hi, can you tell me what English class I'm in? I know it's next period," said Ava when it was her turn.

"Last name?"

"Sackett."

Mrs. Gusman's fingers flew over the keyboard. "A. Sackett, Palmer, room W106."

"Thanks," said Ava with a big grin. She and Jack were in the same class! She sent him a quick text to tell him that, but he didn't answer. No surprise—they weren't allowed to text in class, and the first bell had already rung.

The second bell rang just as she walked into Ms. Palmer's classroom. She scanned the room for an empty desk and saw that there was one— right next to Jack. He was smiling that half smile at her. He'd saved her a seat!

"I'm sorry I'm late," she said to the teacher as she slid into her desk.

Ms. Palmer glanced down at her clipboard and furrowed her brow. "Your name?"

"Ava Sackett."

The rest of the class was a pretty standard

first-day-of-English class. Ms. Palmer passed out textbooks, sternly admonished everyone to cover their books that night and to refrain from writing in them, and outlined her expectations about the writer's notebooks they were going to be maintaining. Then toward the end of class, she passed out the first book they would be reading: *White Fang*.

The title was certainly promising, Ava thought, although the picture of the dog howling at the moon on the cover was somewhat of a letdown. So it wasn't about vampires or sharks. Ava opened to the first page and scanned the very small text with a sinking feeling.

"Please read the first three chapters tonight and write a short response in your writer's notebook," said Ms. Palmer. "And be prepared tomorrow, or any day, for a pop quiz—I need to make sure you're keeping up. This is a wonderful book, but not an easy read, so it's essential not to fall behind. But I'm sure no one in this class will have a problem with that." She smiled at them just as the bell rang.

CHAPTER FOUR

Ava had some trouble finding her social studies class, and when she got there, most kids were already sitting down. She didn't know a single person, but everyone looked up at her as she walked in. Did they know somehow that she was Coach Sackett's daughter, or was she just being super paranoid? There was one girl who hadn't bothered to look up, though—she was sitting quietly at her desk, reading a book with a knight and a dragon on the cover.

Ava sat down next to her, and then the girl did look up and smile at her. It was a genuine, friendly smile. Ava's instincts about people were rarely wrong, and she instantly liked this girl, from the colorful beads at the bottom of her braids to her funky black-and-white cowboy boots.

"I'm Kylie," she said, holding out a hand for Ava to shake. She had an interesting ring on every finger, and her nails were painted different colors—the same colors as the beads in her hair.

"I'm Ava," said Ava, relieved not to have to mention what her last name was.

Kylie's handshake was firm. "You're not from Texas, are you?"

"Um, no, I'm new," said Ava. "How did you know?"

"Lucky guess. Plus, you have a New England Patriots sticker on your notebook."

"Yeah, I guess that's kind of a giveaway," Ava said, smiling.

"You look athletic, too," Kylie said. "What sports do you play? Wait. Let me guess. Are you a runner?"

"I play football," replied Ava automatically. "And basketball, and soccer," she added quickly. She realized that saying she played football could come across as a little strange—after all, usually only boys played football. Then again, Kylie looked like the sort of person who would appreciate someone who was unconventional.

Kylie nodded without missing a beat. "I like that. My sister is a cheerleader at the high school, so I've been to plenty of games. It's not really my thing, though. I have trouble following the rules. So where in New England are you from?"

"Just outside of Boston," said Ava, laughing a little. Kylie practically talked at Alex's pace!

Kylie's eyes sparkled. "I went to Boston this summer!" she exclaimed, bouncing up and down in her seat. "We went to the aquarium and rode in the swan boats. And I had my first New England clam chowder. It was sooo good!"

Ava laughed. Kylie's enthusiasm was infectious. "I love the aquarium too," she agreed.

Their teacher, Mr. Antonucci, clapped his hands to get people's attention, and class began.

Their first task was to partner up and fill out a worksheet about the history of Texas. Kylie and Ava shared a computer station.

"State bird," Ava read off the worksheet.

"Mockingbird," said Kylie, without even doing an Internet search. She opened her notebook and started sketching a bird.

"State flower," said Ava.

"Bluebonnet," said Kylie. Her pen performed a series of loopy maneuvers, and a pretty flower appeared. Ava was impressed.

"Bluebonnet? Really?" asked Ava. "I would have said the yellow rose. Isn't there a song about the yellow rose of Texas?"

"There is, but it's the bluebonnet, trust me."

Ava wrote that down and then looked up. "Guess I chose the right partner."

"You sure did, pardner," said Kylie. She smiled as she added little leaves to her flower.

Ava smiled too. She'd hardly been talking to Kylie for five minutes, and she already felt comfortable around her. Like she did with Charlie, her best friend back in Boston. She hadn't felt that way about anyone in Texas yet . . . well, except for Jack. But the slightly twisty feeling that developed in her stomach when he smiled prevented her from feeling totally comfortable around him too.

"Have you ever ridden a horse?" asked Kylie, interrupting Ava's thoughts.

"Not since I was little. I don't think it counts that I was led around a corral when I was four," admitted Ava.

"No, that doesn't really count. But it's a start! Anyway, I live on a ranch—you should come over and I'll teach you how to ride."

Ava grinned. "I'd love that."

When the twins got home from school that afternoon, they found a note from their mother waiting for them. Mrs. Sackett would be firing at the kiln late, so the twins were supposed to prepare dinner and walk Moxy. Alex got to work chopping veggies for lasagna, and Ava put her shoes back on to take an eager Moxy outside.

Coach and Tommy arrived in silence a few hours later. Coach went to take a shower, but Tommy gave Ava a discreet thumbs-up before going upstairs. "The info session was great!" he said. "I was, like, thirty seconds late to practice, so Coach is mad, but it was worth it!"

Their mom came home just as Ava was pulling the lasagna out of the oven. Alex tossed the salad. Moxy leaped up to greet Mrs. Sackett, her tail wagging her whole back end as though they hadn't seen each other in months.

"Down, girl," said Mrs. Sackett.

Moxy sat, her tail thumping loudly on the linoleum floor.

"Coach and Tommy just got home," Ava reported. "They're taking showers and then coming down to set the table."

"Thank you, girls, for taking care of dinner. I can't wait to hear all about your first days!" Mrs. Sackett set her bag down and leaned against the counter. She had a smudge of dried clay on her nose and some green paint in her hair.

They heard Coach heading down the front stairs. He walked in, freshly showered and smelling of shaving cream, and kissed Mrs. Sackett gently on the forehead.

"Long day, hon?"

"Yes, I'm exhausted," said Mrs. Sackett. "I've forgotten what it's like to do this full-time!" She sank into a chair and smiled gratefully as Ava handed her a large glass of iced tea. Moxy sidled over and put her head on Mrs. Sackett's lap, hoping to be petted.

"I was firing all afternoon," said Mrs. Sackett, her hand now stroking Moxy's glossy head. "And I just found out there's a PTA meeting this Wednesday and I am very much expected to be there. Plus, a reporter from the paper called and asked me for quotes about our family life." She took a long gulp of tea. "Did you remember to stop by the vet for Moxy's medicine, sweetie?"

Coach grimaced. "I'm sorry, hon," he said. "Practice ran late and . . ." He shook his head.

"I just forgot all about it," he admitted.

Mrs. Sackett sighed wearily. "It's okay. I'll go in the morning, before I go to the studio."

Coach hung his head. Ava and Alex exchanged a look.

Later that evening, after Ava had finally finished her social studies reading, she climbed into bed with *White Fang,* her dictionary, and her writer's notebook. She opened to the first page of the book.

> Dark spruce forest frowned on either side the frozen waterway. The trees had been stripped by a recent wind of their white covering of frost, and they seemed to lean toward each other, black and ominous, in the fading light. A vast silence reigned over the land. The land itself was a desolation, lifeless . . .

Ava's mind wandered. She thought about her mom and dad, and how stressed they both seemed. She thought about Tommy, and his feelings about football. Would he ever consider quitting the team? How would Coach respond?

> . . . desolation, lifeless, without movement, so lone and cold that the spirit of it was not even that of sadness. . . .

Her eyes drooped. Why was it so hard to concentrate? The text was small, the language was flowery, and the sentences were so long. Plus, who cared about the landscape? Why couldn't the author get to the fun part, which presumably was a dog or a wolf named White Fang? Was she the only person with this concentration problem? She thought about Jack. Had he breezed through the chapters? Then she thought about Alex. She wished she had Alex's powers of concentration.

"Stop," she said out loud, shaking her head quickly back and forth to wake herself up. "Concentrate."

But the next thing she knew, it was morning. She'd fallen asleep with her light on. Her book had slipped to the floor, and she hadn't read the first page, let alone started the writing assignment.

CHAPTER FIVE

Alex loved Ms. Torres, her English teacher, for her sense of style. She was young and pretty, with full lips and large dark eyes. And two days in a row she'd worn very fashionable outfits. Today she had on a red shift dress and matching red patent leather flats. She also had a lovely, lilting laugh. The downside of English class with Ms. Torres was that it looked like it was going to be a little slow moving. They only had to read one chapter of *Johnny Tremain* per night, and it was not a complex book.

At the start of today's class, Ms. Torres gave them a pop quiz on the reading. Then they passed their quiz to the person behind them and graded their partner's quiz during a guided discussion. As it happened, Corey was sitting behind Alex.

That was the upside to the class. A very good-looking, very twinkly-eyed upside. Not only was Corey in this class, but so was Emily. By some miracle, Alex, Corey, and Emily also shared the same math class. But the difference was Lindsey was also in math with Ms. Kerry. And Alex had found that Emily acted differently when Lindsey was around.

"You got a hundred and five with the extra credit," said Corey as he passed Alex back her quiz. "Impressive."

Alex could feel herself blushing. Was he making fun of her? Did he think she was a big nerd? Alex knew what her mom would say if she knew what Alex was thinking. Mrs. Sackett had always emphasized the importance of being proud of her intelligence and told her never to hide or mask it for the sake of a boy. That was easy for her to say. The fact was, Alex was a nerd. How many other seventh graders were spending their free time studying SAT vocab words?

"That's so great, Alex!" said Emily, who seemed genuinely impressed. Then she leaned in a little closer. "A few of us are going to the mall on Saturday," she whispered. "Want to come? Like around eleven?"

Alex beamed. Her first social invitation of the school year! "I'd love to!" she said.

Ms. Torres cleared her throat.

"I'll text you with the plan once I find out what it is," said Emily quickly.

Alex felt giddy with happiness. She was on her way to being accepted by the popular crowd. And once she was in, she'd help guide Ava into it as well, just as she'd done back in Massachusetts.

But Emily wasn't quite so friendly in math class the next period. She chatted away with Alex as they walked between classrooms together, but once they got there, Emily sat in the only seat next to Lindsey. The day before, there'd been two free seats, but today the second one was occupied by a new kid—probably a transfer from another math section. That left Alex no choice but to sit halfway across the room, next to a kid with his head down on the desk, evidently asleep. Corey leaned over from a few desks away in the same row and grinned at her.

Ms. Kerry wrote a complex equation on the board:

$$343 - 49 \div 7 \times 6^2 + 12$$

"Alex," said Ms. Kerry. "Can you help us to demonstrate order of operations? How would you work this out?" She beckoned Alex up to the board.

Alex glanced at Corey, who gave her an encouraging nod.

She moved to the whiteboard and quickly did the calculations. "You'd first square the six to give you thirty-six. Then you'd divide the forty-nine by seven, and that would give you seven. Then you'd need to multiply the seven by the thirty-six, which would give you two hundred fifty-two, so then it's three hundred forty-three minus two hundred fifty-two plus twelve. And then you'd do the subtraction and the addition to give you"—she calculated quickly—"an answer of one hundred three."

"Very nice! And what if I inserted parentheses around the first two numbers?" Ms. Kerry added parentheses to the equation and then stepped back again. "Would that change your answer?"

"Well, sure," said Alex eagerly. "Because you'd have to do the operation within the parentheses first, rather than dividing the forty-nine by the seven, so the answer would be"—her marker flew—"fifteen hundred twenty-four."

"Excellent!" Ms. Kerry beamed. "And if you group the forty-nine and the seven, would that change the answer?"

"No, because you would do the division first anyway, regardless of whether there were parentheses or not. So the answer would still be one hundred three."

Ms. Kerry's smile broadened. "Lovely work, Alex. You may sit down."

As Alex turned toward her desk, proud of herself and basking in Ms. Kerry's praise, she caught sight of Corey's furrowed brow, staring through half-closed eyes at the calculations Alex had just done in her neat, pretty handwriting. And she saw Lindsey and Emily exchange a look. What did that look mean? Did they think she was showing off?

Alex felt an uneasy awareness bubble to the surface. Emily had seemed so much nicer in English than in math class. It had to be because Lindsey was present. But what had she done wrong? At her last school, it had definitely been cool to be smart. There were a lot of smart kids who were popular. Was it different here? She vowed not to raise her hand for the rest of class.

When the bell rang, she felt a tap on her shoulder. It was Corey.

"Hey. You were awesome up there," he said. "I don't think I could have answered Ms. Kerry's questions like you did if my life depended on it."

Alex glowed. "It was no big deal," she said. "We studied order of operations at the end of last year, and I brushed up a little on them over the summer." She picked up her backpack, which was now quite heavy, and Corey helped her hike it up onto her shoulder. *Not just gorgeous, but also thoughtful!* Alex mused.

"Hey, you know, you should totally sign up for the math team at the Activities Fair on Friday," he said, moving in step with her toward the door of the classroom. "I'm sure they could really use you."

"Thanks," she said, feeling her cheeks flush. "I was planning to sign up for a whole bunch of stuff, actually. What I really want, though, is to be in the student government."

"That makes a lot of sense," said Corey, nodding. "You could totally be the class president even."

"Really?" she asked breathlessly. "You think I could win?"

"Definitely. You're smart. You're organized. You're nice. You're pre—" He stopped himself and blushed to the roots of his hair.

Alex blushed too. Then she looked over his shoulder and saw Lindsey glaring at the two of them. Her elation deflated like a popped balloon. She muttered good-bye to Corey and hurried from the classroom, her face burning hot. She'd need to keep her distance from Corey when Lindsey was around. It was just too risky to flirt with a guy before she'd established herself socially with the girls.

Ava sat at her desk and stared down at the pop quiz she'd gotten back from Ms. Palmer in English that day. A big red "59" was written across the top. She folded the quiz in half and shoved it into the back of the bottom drawer of her desk. Of course she'd failed. She hadn't done the reading. She'd tried, but this book was just too hard for her, with its old-fashioned writing and long sentences. The one class she had with Jack, and she looked like a total idiot.

She needed to get herself to concentrate before she fell further behind. With a sigh, she pulled out *White Fang* and opened it to where she'd left off the night before.

She'd made it about halfway down the page when she heard a gentle tap, and Coach walked in.

"How's it going, champ?" he asked, pulling up her cushy chair and sinking into it.

"Okay, I guess," she said. "I'm having some trouble concentrating on this book for English."

"I thought I noticed your light on late last night when I passed your room," he said. He held out a hand for the book and peered at the title. "*White Fang*, huh? That's a good book. What do you think?"

"It seems like it could be an exciting story, but I haven't really gotten past the first few pages. The author keeps describing every little thing."

He nodded, flipping through the pages. "I seem to recall we read that in high school, not seventh grade."

Ava shrugged. "My teacher keeps talking about 'students of your caliber,' like we're a classroom full of geniuses. If she has expectations like this in our class, what must they be reading in Alex's accelerated English class? *War and Peace,* probably. I'm sure Al's already read it."

Coach chuckled.

"Middle school seems a lot harder than elementary school, Coach."

He nodded and put a strong hand on her shoulder. "But you're tough, Ave," he said. "I know how fierce a competitor you can be on the playing field, and you're smart as a whip. You'll do okay. Every good athlete knows the value of hard work."

Ava swallowed and nodded, although secretly she didn't feel so confident. "Well, on the bright side," she said, changing the subject, "I think I've made a new friend. Her name's Kylie—she rides horses and she's really cool."

"That's great."

"And she invited me to her house on Saturday. She lives on a ranch outside of town."

Alex appeared in the doorway. "Hey, Ave, can I talk to you about—Oh! Hey, Daddy!" she said. "I didn't know you were in here."

"I was just leaving," said Coach, yawning and stretching as he stood up. "It's been a long day."

"I know this is a tough week for you, and for

Mom," said Alex. "What with her big order and everything. And next week's going to be even crazier, because of Thursday."

"You're right, sweetheart," he said. "It's a pretty tough stretch, but—wait. Next Thursday? You mean Friday, don't you?"

"No, Thursday. But don't worry. Ava and I will help you with the planning, won't we, Ave?"

He nodded. "Great. Thanks." Then he paused. "So, um. What's happening on Thursday?"

Ava was also baffled. "Yeah. His first football game's Friday, not Thursday."

Alex looked from one of them to the other, as though she wasn't sure if they were kidding. Then she clapped a hand to her brow and shook her head as though it pained her. She took a step into the room and dropped her voice. "Um, guys? Hello? It's Mom and Dad's anniversary next Thursday? Like, their twentieth?"

Coach's jaw dropped open as though it had become completely unhinged. He fell backward into the chair and looked from one girl to the other with a stricken face. "You're right, Alex. It's a week from Thursday. Holy cow. I completely forgot about our anniversary." He massaged his temples. "And your mom has been so overwhelmed lately with the team duties. I need to do something really special for her."

Alex moved briskly toward Ava's bed and shoved the untidy heap of books and papers out of the way so she could sit down. She took out her phone and opened it up to the notebook app. "Don't worry, Daddy. Ava and I will take care of this," she said.

Ava grinned. It was times like these that she loved her sister's efficiency and knack for planning.

"How about a nice romantic dinner for two?" asked Alex. She began typing away, searching the Internet.

"Um, great. Romantic dinner. Sounds perfect, Al."

"Not a barbecue place," Alex said firmly. "Mom only goes to those places because of you and Tommy and your desire for protein in the form of red meat. What about that adorable little French restaurant that we've passed on the way to the stadium?"

Ava moved from her chair and sat next to her sister, looking on with her. "I know which one you mean. It does look cool. I think it's called Le Pain," she said.

Alex giggled. "It's not pronounced 'pain,'" she said. "You pronounce it 'le pehn.' It's French, silly. It means 'bread.'"

"Okay, so, how about there, Coach?" said Ava. "It's fancy, and it's close. You can get to it right after practice. Alex and I can go there after school and make the arrangements and stuff, you know, make sure they know it's a really special evening and to give you a good table."

"And flowers and candles," added Alex.

Coach moved to the bed and took both girls into his strong arms and gave them each a kiss on the head. "You guys are the greatest. I don't know what I'd do without my girls," he said.

"I'm forced to agree, Daddy," said Alex with a grin. "I don't know what you'd do without us either."

CHAPTER SIX

In Ava's English class on Wednesday, Ms. Palmer handed out another pop quiz.

Ava stared down at the page. There were only five questions. They would be five easy questions, if she'd managed to make it through the reading. But she'd fallen asleep again after staring at the same sentence for five minutes. She had no clue who Henry was, whether he was a wolf or a dog or a human, let alone what happened to him at the end of chapter 3. When Ms. Palmer asked them to put their pencils down, Ava turned her quiz over. She had left three of the answers totally blank. She avoided Jack's eye throughout class and hurried from the room as soon as the bell rang, feeling sick to her stomach.

At dinner that night, Ava considered telling her mom and dad about her struggles in school. But the conversation swirled around the PTA meeting Mrs. Sackett had just attended, and Ava didn't want to make her mother more upset than she already was.

"I was swarmed," Mrs. Sackett said. "Even when I had nothing to say, they called on me and asked me for my input on pretty much every item on the agenda."

"You're a rock star, Mom," said Tommy, pronging another piece of grilled chicken and depositing it on his plate.

"Why would they care what I think about whether the basketball team has orange or white piping on their new uniform shorts? Or whether the refreshment stand at the football game should add veggie burgers to the menu?"

"Ooh, they definitely should!" said Alex. Mrs. Sackett gave her a look. "Sorry."

"But that's nice, honey," said Coach, a hopeful tone in his voice. "That they look up to you. Isn't it?"

"Sure, I suppose, but I don't know what makes me qualified to be in charge of all this. There are plenty of impressive parents in these meetings," Mrs. Sackett continued. "April Cahill is a surgeon, and Dion's mom is an attorney, and I even met a dad who works at the local TV station as a sports broadcaster."

"So there are people you like?" Ava asked. She and her mom were so much alike, often quiet and reserved. Ava knew Mrs. Sackett had left some good friends behind in Massachusetts— she hoped her mom could find some good friends here, like she'd found Kylie.

"There are a few people I like," she admitted. "But I feel this pressure to be so outgoing and authoritative, and that's just not my personality. I'm not sure I'm up for this challenge, Michael."

"Mom, you have to be up for it! For my sake!" Alex cried. "Student elections are just around the corner, and the more that you do, the better I look."

Tommy snorted. Ava sighed.

"Alex, honey, you don't need your mother's help to get yourself elected into the student government," said Coach. "Your classmates would be crazy not to vote for you."

"Oh, and one other thing," said Mrs. Sackett. "Somehow I got roped into baking twelve dozen cookies for the Activities Fair this Friday night.

I don't even remember agreeing to it, but then at the end of the meeting they reminded me about it. Everyone looked so excited that I was doing it that I just couldn't bring myself to say I wouldn't."

"We'll all help you," said Alex quickly.

Ava's heart sank. She hated baking cookies.

"Won't we?" Alex said, more as a threat than a question, looking around the dinner table.

Coach had just taken a drink of his water. He froze midswallow, and then gulped. "Sweetie, Tommy and I have practice on Friday. You know that."

Mrs. Sackett stood up. Her lower lip trembled. "I'm not even a good baker," she said in a high voice that Ava had never heard before. "I didn't sign up for this, Michael. I don't have time for my job, for my family, or for myself."

Coach stood up too and went around the table to take both of her hands in his. "Honey, I totally understand your frustration," he said quietly. "But my job, my role here in town, they depend a lot on your relationship with the town."

Mrs. Sackett nodded and grasped his hands for a moment. "I know. I just—I need some time to—to adjust, Michael." She left the room.

The dinner table was quiet, except for Tommy, who had just taken a large bite of salad. He paused midcrunch, mouth bulging, looking guilty.

Alex broke the silence. "Don't worry, Daddy," she said brightly. "Ave and I will help her bake cookies, right, Ave?"

"Sure," said Ava weakly. She studied Coach's face and noticed that he had tiny worry lines around his eyes. She felt almost as bad for him as she did for her mother.

"And we'll make your anniversary dinner the best ever, right, guys?"

Tommy and Ava nodded vigorously.

Coach's mouth was set in a grim line. "Thanks, kids."

That night Ava fell asleep after just three pages of *White Fang*.

On Thursday she got back the previous day's pop quiz. There wasn't even a grade on it; in large red letters across the top of the paper, Ms. Palmer had written "SEE ME!"

But when the bell rang, Ms. Palmer was bent

over another student, answering a question. Ava glided out of the classroom, like a fish underwater, without getting stopped.

Ms. Palmer caught up with her before the end of the school day. "Ava Sackett!" she called as Ava was emerging from social studies with Kylie. Kylie gave her an *uh-oh* look and walked away.

"Did you see my note on your quiz?" asked Ms. Palmer, staring at Ava over her half-glasses.

"Um, yeah, sorry, had to get to my locker," Ava mumbled, looking down at her green sneakers.

"Ava, I'm baffled by your uneven work," said Ms. Palmer, not unkindly. "You are clearly very bright, and you say insightful things when called on in class discussions, but you don't appear to be keeping up with the outside reading. Is everything all right at home?"

Ava thought about the sort-of fight her parents had had the night before, but she nodded. "Everything's fine," she said. "I just . . . I guess I just have trouble concentrating sometimes."

"What do you mean, exactly?" asked Ms. Palmer.

"I don't know . . . my mind just sort of wanders when I try to do the reading," Ava replied truthfully. "I've been trying really hard, but . . ." Her voice trailed off as she remembered Coach's pep talk from the night before. "I just have to try harder. And I will, I promise."

Ms. Palmer nodded thoughtfully. "Thanks for your honesty. You know, I'm going to recommend to Mrs. Hyde, the learning specialist, that you participate in after-school study until you can improve on your homework performance," she said. "Why don't you try it out today, to see what you think?"

Before Ava could respond to say she had to do something after school, the bell rang.

"Go on to class," said Ms. Palmer. "We can talk more about this later."

Ava scurried away, wondering how this after-school study thing would work. She was supposed to meet Alex to go to Le Pain after school today. And very soon, football tryouts would start.

CHAPTER SEVEN

"You're late," said Alex. She closed her math book and stood up.

She hadn't meant it in a mean way, more of a concerned way.

She was worried about Ava; her sister seemed even more flustered and distracted than usual lately.

"I know, I'm sorry. I had to go check out an after-school study thing, which felt an awful lot like detention to me."

Alex had already started down the school steps, but at Ava's words, she turned around. "You had detention?"

"No," said Ava quickly. "I said it felt like detention."

"Are you in trouble academically?" asked Alex, alarmed.

"No!" Ava said more emphatically. "It's just a study group, that's all. Come on. Let's hustle before they have to start setting up for dinner and stuff."

Alex's mind snapped back to their to-do list. "The good thing is we can walk to Le Pain from here," she said. "Although it is a zillion degrees out and I *was* having the world's best hair day."

Le Pain was midway down an otherwise unassuming stretch of stores, two blocks from the high school. They stopped in front of the restaurant.

A few small tables were set up on the sidewalk, although it was too hot to even think about sitting outside. Alex loved the looks of the plum-colored wooden door and the quaint small-paned windows. "It's right out of Paris!" she said excitedly.

Ava pulled open the heavy door. A little bell tinkled, and a cool rush of air greeted them. Inside, it was hushed, the dim light a relief after the heat and glare from outside.

"May I 'elp you?" asked an elegantly dressed older woman. She wore a beautifully cut yet simple navy sheath and a necklace of blue and silver-gray baubles that looked so perfect Alex resisted a strong impulse to take out her phone and snap a picture so she could copy the look.

"We'd like to make a reservation," both girls said at the same time.

The woman smiled. "You are twins, *non*?"

"Yes," the two girls answered together. All three laughed.

Alex explained to the woman about their parents' upcoming anniversary. "We'd like to reserve a special table for them," she said. "With candles and flowers and everything. For next Thursday at six thirty." The girls had already spoken with Coach about ending practice promptly at six.

"We will take very good care of your parents," the woman assured them. "I am Madame Nicole, the co-owner, and my 'usband is the chef. We will prepare a special *amuse-bouche* for them, and perhaps a cake for dessert?"

The girls agreed that those would be wonderful, and Alex made a mental note to look up what an "amooz-boosh" was. As they turned to leave, Ava stopped, her hand on the heavy door. "Oh, and by the way?" she said to Madame Nicole. "We'd appreciate if no one knew about the reservation."

Madame Nicole's perfectly arched eyebrows rose in question.

"Because, see, our dad is the coach of the football team," Alex said hastily. "And, well, a lot of people in the town like to talk to him when he's out in public, and we really want our parents to have a quiet evening, just the two of them."

Madame Nicole smiled. "I quite understand," she said. "We will look forward to seeing them!"

Back outside, Ava turned to Alex. "What about music?" she asked.

Alex blinked at her. "Music?"

"Yeah, you know how in old movies there's always a dude who comes to the table and serenades the couple with a violin? Maybe we could find a dude to play violin."

"First of all," said Alex, "we don't know any 'dudes' who play violin. And second of all, we don't have the money to pay for something like that. And third of all, we're trying to keep this dinner quiet. If word got out that Daddy is going to be there the night before the first game of the season, chances are the newspapers would be there to pester him!"

"Tommy might know someone," persisted Ava. "He's part of . . . I mean, I think he knows other people who play instruments. I'm going to ask him."

"Okay, fine," said Alex. Suddenly she stopped short.

"What's up, Al?"

"A present," said Alex. "You know Daddy won't remember to get Mom a present, right?"

"Oh, you're right," said Ava.

"And she's probably got something really special for him. Remember that year she made him that amazing ceramic football that he loved? So we have to think of something."

The girls walked in silence for a few more paces before Alex stopped again and clutched her sister's arm. "I just thought of the perfect present," she said to Ava, her eyes shining. She told Ava her idea.

"It is perfect," agreed Ava. "I can't wait until he gets home so we can tell him the plan."

But Coach was late getting home for dinner that night.

"He stayed behind with the other coaches to watch film," Tommy reported as he slid into his chair, freshly scrubbed from his postpractice shower, and heaped two pork chops onto his plate.

"I'll put aside some dinner for him," said Mrs. Sackett wearily. She had dark circles under her eyes and barely touched her dinner. The girls exchanged worried looks.

After the dishes were done, Alex and Ava disappeared into their own rooms to do their homework. It wasn't until much later, after she'd turned out her light, that Alex heard her father's tires crunching in the driveway. She knew her mom had long since gone to bed. She heard some bangs and clanks in the kitchen—he was probably heating up his dinner, she figured.

The last thing Alex was aware of before she drifted off to sleep was the smell of cookies baking.

CHAPTER EIGHT

The twins came home from school on Friday to a steaming kitchen and a very frazzled mother.

"Hi, girls—ow!" said Mrs. Sackett, quickly banging the oven door closed. "That's the second time I've burned myself in half an hour," she said, sucking on the back of her hand. "Have I mentioned that I am not a baker?"

"Yes," said Alex. "But Mom, I appreciate what you're doing. It's really important to Daddy, and it's fantastic how well you're carrying out your duty as the coach's wife."

Ava frowned at her sister and moved into the kitchen to help their mother shovel warm cookies onto the cooling rack. "You make it sound like this is 1955, Alex," she said. "This must stink, doing all this PTA stuff," she said to their mom. "When there's so much other stuff you could be doing."

Mrs. Sackett wiped her forehead with the back of her hand, leaving a streak of flour behind. "It's not like your father is kicking back and watching TV," she said. "He's working hard too. In fact, when he got home late last night, he stayed up past midnight and baked as many batches as he could stay awake for."

"That's so sweet!" said Alex excitedly. "And we'll help you with the rest, won't we, Ave?"

Ava was already stacking cooled cookies onto plates to make room for the next batch. It was hot, despite the blasting air-conditioning, and her short hair stuck out in spikes. Alex made a mental note to try to interest her sister in stylish headbands. They'd look so cool and sophisticated on her.

Coach and Tommy returned from practice just as Alex was taking the final batch of cookies out of the oven.

"Mom and Ava are upstairs getting ready," she said to them. "And I'm about to head up too. There's sandwich stuff for dinner because we're heading off to the Activities Fair. Are you going to come too, Daddy?"

Coach shook his head. He looked tired. "I better not," he said. "I'll just be ambushed, and this evening is for you girls, not me."

He headed upstairs to confer with Mrs. Sackett, leaving Alex and Tommy alone in the kitchen. In a conspiratorial whisper, Alex reported on their progress with the anniversary dinner.

"Ava wants a violin player to serenade them at the table," she said dubiously. "She thinks you might know someone?"

Tommy was thoughtful. "I just might," he said. "I'll get back to you on that."

Ava, Alex, and Mrs. Sackett pulled into a space in the vast Ashland Middle School parking lot, which was already a sea of cars.

"So you girls know what you're going to sign up for, right?" asked Mrs. Sackett. "Because honestly, I'm exhausted. I have to work the bake sale table for an hour, and then I'd love to get out of here, if you'll be ready. I think trying to field questions about Daddy's offensive strategies is going to make me even more tired!"

Alex giggled. "We'll be fast, Mom," she said.

"I have my list: student government, newspaper, debate team, math club, model UN, and community service."

"Not the Human Genome Code-Cracking Club too?" teased Ava.

Alex sniffed. "All these clubs are good résumé builders. Besides, I have to have backups if I don't win the election for class president."

"Well, I'll be done in five minutes," said Ava. "I'm just signing up for one thing."

As they got out of the car, Mrs. Sackett handed each of the girls a heavy shoe box, which they'd helped line with wax paper and fill with cookies. "Just leave these on the refreshment table and you're free."

They entered the double doors leading into the gym. Alex was overwhelmed by the vast crowd of kids and parents roaming from table to table, talking and laughing. Representatives for the activities were stationed at each table to answer questions and direct sign-ups.

After dropping off her box of cookies, Ava set off to find the football table and was soon absorbed into the crowd. Alex looked around, wondering what she should sign up for first, and spotted the cheerleading table, and right next to it, the marching squad table. There was Lindsey, and there was Emily, both surrounded by hordes of laughing, chatting girls. She thought fleetingly of signing up for cheerleading tryouts, but quickly dismissed it. She was too uncoordinated, and at AMS the cheerleading was top-notch. As fun as it looked, Alex knew she would only humiliate herself if she tried out.

She scanned the crowd for Corey. There he was, sitting at the football table, looking gorgeous and jock-y. Her heart gave a leap. Had he seen her? He wasn't facing her direction.

Oh. And there was Ava, also at the football table, talking to him. *Is she really going to sign up for football?* Alex thought. It was one thing when it was Pee Wee football in Boston, but middle school football in Texas? She wondered how big of a deal this would be, and how big of a deal Ava could handle. . . .

Ava wrote her name on the clipboard. She was really signing up for football.

She was aware that the boys standing around the table had gone quiet. That they were all staring at her as she put the pen down and straightened up. At least Corey was smiling at her.

"Awesome," he said. "What position do you play?"

"Kicker," she replied. "At least, that's what I was on my old team."

"That's a position that requires a lot of finesse," he said. "And we can sure use some finesse on this team, if you look around."

Someone threw a crumpled napkin at him, and the tension near the table eased. Ava felt a swell of gratitude toward Corey. She headed off into the crowd, feeling them staring at the back of her as she did so. She knew they were talking about her. About the new girl who thought she could play football.

Sometimes Texas felt like a foreign country. It wasn't like a girl on a football team was exactly an everyday thing back in Massachusetts, of course, but there, after the first few days of practice, everyone sort of got used to the idea, and it wasn't such a big deal. Would the same thing be true here, where football itself was so much more important? She hoped so. But she somehow doubted it.

Someone whacked her over the head with a rolled-up poster. She turned. It was Jack.

"I hear you signed up for football," he said, grinning at her mischievously.

"News travels fast," she said. "I only just signed up forty-two seconds ago."

"Yeah, well, it's going to be on the eleven o'clock news tonight."

"Come on, seriously?" she scoffed. "Is it really something people are talking about? Should I be freaked out?"

"Nah," he said, shaking his head. "I was just talking to a couple of guys on the team and they know I"—he paused, considering his words—"they know I know you," he finished.

What had he been about to say? Ava wondered to herself. Had he been about to say "they know I like you?" She shook her head almost imperceptibly. That was dumb. Of course he didn't *like* like her. Theirs was a mutually respectful sports friendship. Besides, her life was complicated enough.

"Um, I think your sister is over there waving at you," said Jack, gesturing with his chin.

Ava followed his gaze. Alex was standing by the stage, giving Ava a look, one that Ava knew meant her twin needed to talk to her.

"Yeah, we probably have to go rescue our mother from the bake sale table," she said to him. "See you later."

Ava could feel her cheeks getting warm as she left him. This was totally dumb. She already had a kind of, sort of thing with her friend Charlie, or at least, she had when she left Boston. They'd been texting each other pretty often before school had started, but lately, life had gotten busier, and the texting had been less frequent.

She joined Alex near the stage. "Everything okay?" she asked her sister.

"Yes and no. I keep getting these looks from Lindsey, and I think it's because Corey might just possibly like me. And I might just possibly like him."

"No, really?" asked Ava with a hint of sarcasm, but it was lost on Alex.

"Well, I'm not positively positive yet. It is true—no, it is incontrovertible—that he is really cute."

"Does that mean true?"

"Yes. But the thing is, I feel like if I let on that I like him, that's going to make Lindsey mad, and I really want to stay on her good side, so

I've been trying to avoid him since we got here. But he keeps showing up when I don't expect him to and—ow! Why did you just kick me?"

Ava raised her eyebrows meaningfully. Alex's blood froze, and she turned oh-so-casually to her left.

Corey was standing right next to her.

"Hey," he said to Alex.

"H-h-hey!" said Alex breathily, her face turning bright pink to the tips of her ears.

Ava tried to sidle away, but she was semi-trapped between the corner of the stage and a French Club sign-up table. She turned toward the table and pretended to be engrossed in a French menu, but she kept her ears open.

"So, like, I assume you're going to the game next Friday?" Corey asked. Then quickly he added, "Because, I mean, obviously you are because your dad's like, the coach."

Ava turned slightly to look at him out of the corner of her eye. He was blushing! He was staring down at his shoes with his shoulders hunched and his hands plunged into his pockets. It looked like he really did like Alex. That was fine with Ava; now that she knew Corey was supportive of their dad's team—and Ava playing football!—she approved of him.

"So, pretty much everyone in our grade goes to Sal's Pizzeria after the game? And I was wondering if you wanted to, like, hang out there after too?"

"Like a date?" Alex blurted out.

Ava cringed inwardly.

Corey was looking right and left, as though seeking an escape route in case he had to sprint away suddenly. "Well, sort of. Everyone is going to be there too but, like, yeah, I guess it's like a date."

There was an excruciating silence. Ava ducked down to the table, trying to look like she was completely absorbed in the sign-up list for a bus trip to an upcoming production of Albert Camus's *La Peste*.

"Um, well, uh, maybe that would be fun," stammered out Alex. "I just need to, um, check with my parents, because it's my dad's first game and all. I don't know if we're doing some family thing or something."

"Okay, cool," said Corey, and darted away as quickly as he had appeared.

"Ava!" hissed Alex. "That was so—I was so—awkward! And what if Lindsey saw?" She whipped her head around to look at the cheer-leading table. Sure enough, Lindsey was staring at her.

Ava followed her sister's gaze. This time, the look on Lindsey's face was less angry and more . . . hurt. Ava almost felt sorry for her.

Ava sighed. "Come on. Let's go rescue Mom from the bake sale."

CHAPTER NINE

"Her name's Layla," said Kylie. "Isn't she beautiful?"

"Yes," said Ava, swallowing. "Beautiful in a very large way."

Kylie laughed and patted the horse's flank. "She's ten years old and gentle as a lamb, I promise. She's the best kind of horse to ride if you're not used to riding."

"Like I said, I haven't been on a horse since I was a little kid, at the county fair. So it's an understatement to say I'm not used to riding."

Layla tossed her head and snorted, as though she were dismissing Ava's fears.

"Put your foot here," said Kylie. "I'll give you a boost up. Don't worry, you'll get the hang of it."

She helped Ava put her foot in the stirrup. With a little shove from Kylie, Ava pulled herself high into the saddle and swung her other leg around until she was sitting on Layla's back.

She looked down at Kylie and felt a thrill of excitement, mixed with a healthy dose of terror. "I'm so high up!" she said.

"Yep, she's a quarter horse. She's a big girl. But just hold the reins like I told you, and she'll follow me and Chester, I promise."

"Thanks for inviting my sister, too," said Ava. "Sorry she couldn't make it, but she'd already made plans to go to the mall today. Which is not my idea of a fun way to spend a Saturday."

"I agree," said Kylie. "I only go to the mall when it's absolutely necessary. I like clothes, but I'd rather make my own or go to a thrift store."

Ava watched Kylie swing herself nimbly into her horse's saddle. She sat high, her back straight, her shoulders squared.

"How long have you been riding?" Ava asked as Layla plodded up alongside Chester.

"Since I was teeny," said Kylie with a laugh. "This has been my family's ranch for generations. Did you know that one out of six cowboys on the American frontier was African American? I have riding in my veins."

"That's so cool," said Ava. "I like that you're a cowboy. Because speaking of things you don't see girls doing every day, I just signed up for the football team."

"How'd that go?" asked Kylie. "Did you get any pushback?"

"Not really," said Ava, patting Layla's glossy neck. "The boys mostly just whispered as I walked away."

"Well, good for you for doing it," said Kylie. "People around here have some pretty set ideas about how things ought to work. I think it's great to shake things up a little."

She made a little clicking sound, and Chester took two prancing steps. "Now, grip Layla tight with your knees. I know how to ride both Western and English style, but I thought Western would be easier for you. The saddle's a little easier to sit in, and we can trot without posting."

Ava had no clue what Kylie was talking about, but she didn't care. It was exhilarating to be up on the horse. Although she hadn't realized how hard it was to grip the saddle with your knees. She'd probably be a little sore tomorrow.

"I thought we'd be wearing cowboy hats," she said, adjusting her helmet strap a little farther under her chin.

"Nope, helmets are much safer," said Kylie. "Even the best horses can get startled and bolt. Two years ago I got thrown from Chester. We were on a trail, and the horse in front of us threw a rock up and hit him in the chest. He got spooked and bolted. I landed on my head but I was fine, thanks to my helmet."

Ava gulped and gripped the saddle tighter with her knees.

Kylie made a little clicking noise again and flicked the reins almost imperceptibly, and Chester led the way out of the paddock at a gentle pace. Layla followed a nose behind.

"I'm riding!" said Ava. "This is so amazing!" She loved being up high, and feeling the wind on her face. She loved the smell of the leather tack, and the silky feel of Layla's mane.

"You're doing well!" Kylie said over her shoulder. "You're a natural."

"Thanks," said Ava. "I love animals." She patted Layla's neck again. "I wish I could ride Layla all day instead of going to class."

"Having some issues?" Kylie clicked her

tongue, and Chester slowed so that the two horses could ride side by side across the wide, flat grassland.

"Mostly with English," said Ava. "And a little in social studies, when the reading gets boring. But in general, school seems so much harder this year. I'm having concentration problems."

"Are you distracted by anything, or anyone? Maybe . . . Jack Valdeavano? I saw you guys talking at the Activities Fair!"

"What? No! Well, I mean, he's nice and all. I do like him. But I've got this complicated situation with a guy back in Massachusetts . . . it's a long story."

"For the record, Jack's a really great guy," said Kylie, as she turned Chester's nose to the left. Layla tossed her head as though to agree with the decision, and turned and followed in step with Chester. "But what do you mean by 'concentration problems'?"

Ava told Kylie about her struggles with *White Fang*, and her two failed pop quizzes.

Kylie nodded thoughtfully. "Maybe you should talk to the teacher, or your parents. Because I hate to break this to you, but you have to maintain a C average to be allowed to play sports."

That was a blow. "Oh," said Ava. "I didn't know that. I went to after-school study hall a couple of times, but I couldn't concentrate there, either. Maybe I should talk to my mom and dad." She was quiet for a few minutes.

"Want to try a trot?" asked Kylie.

"Okay," said Ava.

"Just sit up straight and keep gripping the saddle," instructed Kylie. "Layla will do what Chester does."

"I'm glad you told me to wear pants," said Ava. "This could be painful with bare legs."

"Yep, but you're doing great. If you get good at this, we'll have to suit you up in chaps," said Kylie. And with a little cluck, she and Chester started off, with Ava and Layla right behind.

"So what's going on with you and Corey?" Emily asked Alex as they strolled through the mall. They were on their way to meet up with a group of girls, some of whom Alex had met and some of whom she didn't know.

"Corey? Oh. Nothing. Nothing at all," said Alex quickly.

"Awww, come on, Alex," Emily wheedled. "Anyone who spends two seconds with the two of you can see you guys like each other."

"They can?" asked Alex anxiously. She stopped in her tracks and turned to face Emily. "Okay, fine. I confess: I do like him. And he even asked me out! But I don't know what to do, because I get the feeling that Lindsey likes him too." Alex paused and tried to gauge Emily's reaction. It was possible she was treading into dangerous waters here—Emily and Lindsey were close. "I just—I don't want to make Lindsey mad at me. Do you know what's going on between them?"

"Come on," said Emily. "We have twenty minutes before we meet up with everyone. I could use a smoothie. Let's sit and talk about this."

A few minutes later they were sitting across a table from each other in the food court—a much fancier food court than Alex had known at the malls back in Massachusetts. Alex had a mango-orange smoothie, and Emily a strawberry-banana.

"So here's the thing," said Emily. "A few years ago, Lindsey's parents and Corey's parents opened a business together. A restaurant. And I think they had some sort of argument over it, and stopped being partners. I think Lindsey's family is now having some money problems."

Alex nodded. "I heard that too."

Emily tossed her long blond hair out of her face and took a sip of her pink smoothie.

Alex took a sip of her smoothie too. She was dying for more information from Emily but didn't want to look desperate.

"Anyway, I guess their parents don't get along anymore. So it got awkward that Lindsey and Corey were sort of going out."

Alex sat back in her chair and regarded Emily. "That does sound awkward," she said.

"I guess last year the strain got to them, and they stopped hanging out. She doesn't really talk about it, but I think you're right—she still likes him. Anyway, I know Lindsey can seem a little . . . mean sometimes, but she really is a good friend. I think it does upset her to see Corey interested in someone else."

"Like me?"

"Yeah, like you." Emily leaned forward and fixed Alex with a serious look. "Do you want my opinion?"

Alex nodded her head vigorously.

"I think Lindsey would eventually get over it

if you started going out with Corey. But if you want to be friends with her, maybe going out with him isn't the best idea in the world."

"That makes sense," said Alex dejectedly. She thought about Corey: his smile, his dimples, how adorably nervous he got around her. But it probably wasn't worth it to make Lindsey mad. "She seems like she already doesn't like me," said Alex, staring miserably into her smoothie cup.

"That's not true," said Emily kindly. "I think she's got other stuff going on. Last year she was one of the best cheerleaders on the AMS team, even as a sixth grader. But now she's saying she might go out for the marching squad instead. I have a feeling it might be a financial thing. Being on the cheerleading squad is expensive."

Alex covered her face in her hands. "That explains why she told me she might not go out for the team," she said. "I had no idea cheerleading was more expensive. And I acted all surprised and stuff. I can't believe how clueless I was." She groaned.

"Don't worry about it," said Emily brightly. She stood up. "Come on. Let's go meet up with the rest of the gang."

CHAPTER TEN

Sunday morning Ava stepped out of bed and almost fell down. Her legs were screaming! She'd never realized how much you had to clench your thigh muscles to stay in the saddle of a horse.

Tommy stopped with his fork midway to his mouth as Ava hobbled into the kitchen. "What's the matter with you?"

Coach was ladling pancake batter onto the hot griddle. He turned and smiled. "She went riding is what's the matter," he said. "Little saddle sore, sweetheart?"

"Just a little," said Ava grumpily, hobbling toward the refrigerator. She pulled out the orange juice and then sank into a chair with a groan.

"Tommy and I were just talking about the game coming up this Friday," said Coach.

"Shocking, I know," added Tommy with a wry grin.

"You guys ready?" asked Ava.

Coach grunted.

"I need to know, because every other person I see asks me if my dad's team is going to beat Mainville," said Ava.

Tommy shrugged. "It depends on how focused PJ is that day," he said. "He's kind of all over the place mentally. Is that fair, Coach?"

Coach nodded. "He's got some growing up to do. He's a great athlete, but he's cocky."

"Well, I hope he's ready," said Tommy, "because Dion's hurting. Dee won't let on, but I think his leg is bothering him. I saw him limping pretty heavily after practice yesterday when he thought no one was around to see him."

Coach pressed his lips together. "I think you might be right, Tom," he said. "But PJ has been looking good. It's his head we've got to contend with."

"Maybe Tommy can be QB," said Ava playfully.

"Oh, yeah, right," said Tommy. "Like that'll ever happen."

"Tom," said Coach, and he had on his serious face. "You're just a sophomore. You're still growing, getting stronger. You have a lot of potential to become a very good QB—more than very good. You've got speed, quickness, agility, and a rock-solid arm. And Dion is showing real promise as our go-to kicker."

Silence descended. Ava watched Tommy slather peanut butter onto a pancake. He rolled it up and ate it in three bites.

"Morning, everyone!" Alex bounced into the kitchen, annoyingly chipper as usual. She looked from Tommy to Coach to Ava and pursed her lips. "You were talking about football, weren't you?"

"Of course, darlin'. But we'll stop. Here's a pancake with your name on it," said Coach, handing her a steaming plate.

Tommy scraped his chair away from the table and brought his plate to the sink. "I'm going over to the church to practice," he said. "The service ended at nine, and the next one doesn't start until noon, so I have a nice chunk of practice time."

After he'd left, Coach took a long sip of coffee and stared into space, deep in thought.

Ava and Alex looked at each other.

"Do you really think Tommy can be a starting quarterback someday?" asked Ava.

Coach set his mug down gently on the table. "He could. Depends on what he wants. I wish he spent as much time thinking about football as he does about piano."

The girls were quiet for a few minutes. Then Alex spoke. "I think we're all set for Thursday, Daddy."

Coach looked up, baffled. "Thursday? The game's Friday."

Alex closed her eyes and sighed. "Your. Anniversary. Dinner."

He jumped as though he'd been poked from behind. "Of course! Right! I knew that!"

Alex leaned forward and whispered into Ava's ear. "Tommy found a violinist for the dinner."

Mrs. Sackett and Moxy bustled into the kitchen from their walk. Even at this early hour, Mrs. Sackett's face was flushed and her hair was escaping from her ponytail. Moxy went straight to her dish and began lapping water noisily, showering everything nearby with droplets.

"Hot already out there, Mom?" asked Alex.

Mrs. Sackett filled a glass of water and gulped

it all down. "Yes," she gasped, setting the glass down.

Coach stood up and enveloped his wife in a bear hug. "Have I ever mentioned how lucky I am?" he crooned into her hair.

Mrs. Sackett looked at the girls over his shoulder, a slightly startled expression on her face. "Um, not recently." She smiled and hugged him back. "It's nice to hear."

Alex laughed when she looked over at her sister and saw a slightly revolted look on her face.

"I think they're cute!" she said.

CHAPTER ELEVEN

Monday afternoon Ava staggered out of after-school study, her mind whirling. Why did she have so much trouble concentrating? It wasn't like she could blame the distracting noises around her, because after-school study was quiet. But somehow a quiet setting made it worse. As she'd sat at her desk, staring down at her social studies textbook, her thoughts had spun out into other thoughts. The page of reading in front of her had grown dim, the letters dancing on the paper. She'd tried switching to English, but after slogging through two pages of *White Fang,* she'd realized she had no idea what she'd just read and had to begin all over again.

After the late bus dropped her off, she stopped at the little park near her house, wishing she had a basketball with her. On the other hand, maybe it was a good thing she didn't—she was still pretty sore from riding on Saturday.

It was nearly five, and the day had finally cooled off. The park was deserted—the kids who usually played there had probably gone home for dinner. She had the little play area to herself, and she sat on a swing, pondering.

It wasn't just that she was feeling more distracted and having trouble concentrating. It was organization, too. Not that that had ever been a strength of hers, but she found moving from class to class so much harder than staying in one classroom all day. She was constantly leaving the book she needed in her locker, or forgetting her homework at home, or losing the assignment sheet. What was wrong with her? Alex seemed to have no trouble adjusting.

After a few minutes, she came to a decision. She would tell her mom and dad about the failed quizzes. She knew they both had a lot on their minds, and her struggles in school were probably the last thing her parents needed right now. But maybe they'd be able to help her switch to some other teacher, one who didn't have such high expectations. Ms. Palmer wasn't mean, but she kept looking at Ava with such pained disappointment. It wasn't exactly helping Ava feel more confident. She stood up, squared her shoulders, and marched home.

When Ava walked into the kitchen, her dad and Tommy were emptying the dishwasher, engaged in a heated discussion.

"Dad, I told you. I'll just be five minutes late, twice a week," said Tommy. His cheeks had two pink spots on them.

Coach's mouth was set in a grim line, and he clanked the plates louder than was necessary.

Mrs. Sackett was on the phone. Alex stood nearby, jumping from one foot to the other, waiting for her mother to get off.

No one acknowledged that Ava was home.

Mrs. Sackett hung up. "That was the *Ashland Times*," she said. "Again. They're running a huge story on you tomorrow, Michael. And they were asking me some very personal questions about our family life. I told them now wasn't a good time because we're about to eat dinner, and they said they'd call back in fifteen minutes."

Ava cleared her throat. "Mom? Dad?" she said

in a low voice. "I wanted to tell you about these two quizzes? In my English class?"

"Mom, I'm sorry about the short notice, but I absolutely have to wear something orange tomorrow because it's the first Spirit Week of the year, and I just noticed two missing buttons on my new shirt and—"

"Give me a second, please, Alex, to talk to your father," said Mrs. Sackett.

"I can't give preferential treatment to my own kid. You know that, Tom," said Coach, who was now placing the silverware into its drawer with considerable force. "You're going to have to make some tough choices here."

Ava set down her backpack. Moxy trotted over to be petted. Her wagging tail banged the metallic garbage can and added a repetitive tympanic boom to the conversation in progress.

Ava tried again. "And I thought maybe you guys could talk to—"

Moxy perked up her ears, barked sharply twice, and then bolted into the living room to look at something outside.

"Fifteen minutes, the reporter said. Like that's how long he's giving us to eat dinner," Mrs. Sackett continued.

"Where am I going to find two orange buttons?" wailed Alex.

"You're my son, Tommy. I have to be harder, not easier, on you," said Coach.

"Mom," Tommy said, craning his neck to peek into the living room. "It looks like Moxy threw up on the carpet."

Ava slipped quietly out of the kitchen.

The next morning Alex got up early to join her mother on her morning walk with Moxy. She loved doing this once in a while—she had always been the earliest riser of the three kids, and she loved the alone time with her mom.

"So is everything going well at school?" Mrs. Sackett asked as they set off down the block. The air was delightfully cool, and the sun had not quite risen in the eastern sky.

"English is pretty boring," said Alex. "I mean, the work part. I like the kids in my class. Especially—" She stopped. She'd almost said, *Especially Corey.* But maybe she was getting too old to share stuff like this with her mom.

Her mom glanced at her sideways but kept

silent. Moxy spotted a small dog on a leash across the street and strained to get closer to it. "Heel, Moxy," said Mrs. Sackett, gently tugging the dog back toward the sidewalk.

But Alex wanted to tell her mom about Corey. "Okay, so there's this guy I like," she blurted out. "His name's Corey."

And then she shared everything. About how Corey had asked her out. And how she knew there was this other girl who liked him too, and she really wanted to be friends with that other girl, but she thought it would cause problems if she, Alex, went out with Corey. And how she had no clue what to do.

Her mom listened and nodded, looking thoughtful. "I think you should follow what your heart tells you, hon," she said when Alex finished. "You're wiser than you might think you are."

"What if I have no idea what my heart is telling me?" asked Alex. "I really like Corey, but I really want to be part of Lindsey's group. I'm completely torn!"

Mrs. Sackett smiled sympathetically. "I can tell you that in my experience, friends usually last longer than crushes do. If this girl is really someone you value as a potential friend, maybe you should follow your instincts, and hold off on rushing into something with Corey."

Alex nodded. Her mom was always so comforting. She put her arm through her mom's and gave her a squeeze. "Thanks, Mom," she said. "I think that's what I'll do."

When they returned from the walk, they found Coach reading the article about himself in the *Ashland Times* with a queasy expression on his face. The article wasn't on the front page of the sports section—it was on the front page of the paper.

"Laur," he said, looking up at Mrs. Sackett over his half-glasses. "Was it necessary to tell them I like to bake?"

Mrs. Sackett laughed, and then hung Moxy's leash on the hook. "You do like to bake, dear. It seemed like a harmless detail. All the other questions felt too personal. I passed on most."

Coach read from the article. "'Coach Sackett's pie crust was legendary back at the Three-County Fair in their former Massachusetts town. His cherry pie won honorable mention two years in a row.'"

"Well, it did!" said Mrs. Sackett. She moved to the sink and filled Moxy's water bowl. "I was flustered," she said, turning around and smiling sheepishly. "The reporter was asking me so many questions, and I was in the middle of about three things and I think I started rambling. I'm really sorry, hon!"

Coach smiled back at her, but when he flipped through several more pages of the paper to where the article continued, he groaned loudly. "Laur! You sent them this picture of me having a tea party with the girls?"

Alex looked over his shoulder. "It's a really sweet picture, Daddy," she said, trying to make it okay, even though she knew it wasn't. "We were only four, right? You look so cute, sitting in that tiny chair with your long legs and holding that little teacup in your two fingers."

Her father glared at her.

She shut her mouth.

"Michael. I know you're trying to come off as a strong, tough leader to the town in the days leading up to your first home game." Mrs. Sackett plunked Moxy's bowl down, sloshing water onto the floor. When she stood up, Alex could see that her eyes were bright and she looked honestly upset that she'd messed up. "The reporter seemed to want me to talk about personal stuff, and these things seemed harmless at the time—I just kind of blathered on without thinking. I'm sorry! You see? I don't think I'm cut out for this." She left the kitchen.

Alex was at a loss for words, which was rare for her. She moved to the coffee machine and filled her father's cup back up, and then set the pot gently back on the burner. He didn't even seem to notice.

In homeroom Mr. Kenerson told Alex to report to the office.

Alex gulped. Was she in trouble? She never got called to the office.

Mr. Kenerson's face was impossible to read. What was the word she'd learned the other day? Inscrutable. That was it. His face was inscrutable.

She picked up her books and left, feeling everyone's curious eyes on her. As she hurried down the empty hall, her heart thudded. What had she done? Was something wrong? Had something happened to her family?

The first person she saw when she walked into the outer office was Ava. She was sitting by herself, wearing a blue football jersey in accidental defiance of Spirit Week—Tuesday was the day to wear orange. Ava looked perplexed but not scared. There was another vocab word that described her face. In her nervousness, Alex's mind hit a metaphorical search button. Stoic. Ava was sitting and looking stoic. Or was it "stoical"? Stoical—bearing hardship or misfortune without complaint.

Ava looked up, still looking stoical.

"What's going on?" hissed Alex, sitting down next to her. "Are we in trouble?"

"Of course we're not in trouble. We haven't done anything wrong," said Ava. She spoke as though she had something in her mouth. Alex saw a bulge in her cheek. "And I don't think it's bad news or anything, because Mrs. Gusman smiled at me when I walked in and offered me candy and showed me a picture of her new baby grandson. These candies are delicious, by the way."

Alex saw her shift the candy to the other side of her mouth.

"She wouldn't be that casual and friendly if

someone in our family was sick or hurt. I don't know what it could be, though," Ava said.

"Sackett girls?" called Mrs. Gusman. "Ms. Farmen is ready for you."

Alex followed Ava into the principal's office. It was light and cheerful, with framed student artwork on the walls and lots of pictures of Ms. Farmen's kids, who looked like they were pretty much grown up.

"Hi, girls," said Ms. Farmen. "Sit. Please." She opened a folder and frowned down at it. "First of all, Mrs. Gusman, our scheduling guru, just informed me that there was some confusion with your names both being 'A. Sackett.' It seems you were placed in each other's English classes. Ava, you were supposed to be in English 101. Alex, you were supposed to be in 101A—that's the accelerated class—based on your test scores. I'm so sorry about this. But we can easily make the switch without disrupting the rest of your schedule. Ava, you will no longer be in Ms. Palmer's class—now you have Mr. Rader, still during sixth period. Alex, you'll have Ms. Palmer, also still during sixth period."

Alex darted a glance at Ava. Relief was written all over her sister's face. No wonder Ava had been having so much trouble with English! She'd been put into the advanced class. And no wonder she, Alex, had found English so easy. Then a thought struck her. If she switched out, she wouldn't have English with Corey anymore. Was that a good thing or a bad thing?

"All right, Alex. You may go," said Ms. Farmen. "I have another matter to discuss with Ava. Please ask Mrs. Gusman to write you a note, as I think the second bell has rung."

Alex thanked her, shot a look at Ava that said "Tell me everything later," and hurried off to her first class.

"Ava, why don't you go wait outside in Mrs. Gusman's office?" said Ms. Farmen. "I'll call you when I'm ready for you."

Ava swallowed, nodded, and left.

And almost ran smack into her parents, who were walking into Mrs. Gusman's office.

Ms. Palmer, Ava's now-former English teacher, was right behind them. Another lady was there too, standing with an armful of thick files.

"Hey there, kiddo," said Coach. "Fancy meeting you here."

CHAPTER TWELVE

Ava didn't have a chance to talk to Alex until after school, when they met at their lockers.

"What happened?" asked Alex, her eyes wide and anxious. "Are you in trouble? Are you expelled?"

"I'm not expelled," said Ava stiffly. "First you think I'm in detention, then you think I'm expelled. Thanks for the vote of confidence, Al."

"But why were Mom and Dad here? And who was that official-looking lady with all the files?"

"That was Mrs. Hyde. She's the school learning specialist." Ava took a deep breath. "They want to test me for ADHD, because of all the trouble I've had concentrating. That stands for attention-deficit/hyperactivity disorder."

Alex's eyes got even bigger. "I know what it stands for, it's just—wow, Ave, this is really serious. I always knew you weren't organized, but I never thought it was a disorder." She talked slowly and quietly; Ava must be really upset.

But Ava smiled calmly and put a comforting hand on Alex's arm. "Me neither," she said. "But it's not the end of the world, Al. Weirdly, I feel kind of relieved. Because it explains a lot of the concentration problems I've been having, and the organizational issues, that kind of thing. It makes me feel better, knowing what the problem is. And Ms. Palmer went on about how brilliant she still thinks I am." Ava rolled her eyes. "So they're going to have something called a PPT—a Planning and Placement Team—and I'm supposed to get tested and stuff."

"When will you know for sure?"

"Within the next few weeks," said Ava. "But everyone seems pretty sure. Mom and Coach already brought up getting me a tutor."

"I could tutor you!" Alex began excitedly. She had always felt helpless when it came to Ava's study habits, but tutoring—that was something she could do! "It'd be perfect!" Alex continued. "We could do it every night after—"

"Hey," interrupted a low voice.

Both girls turned. It was Corey.

Alex jumped. Talk about bad timing. She'd successfully avoided talking to him all day. In math she'd pretended she had a question for Ms. Kerry after the bell rang, just to avoid walking out with him. Out of the corner of her eye she saw Ava move away and pull out her phone, probably to text Charlie about her potential ADHD.

"So," Corey said. "Did you do any more thinking about the Friday plan?" The words came out of his mouth very quickly.

Alex glanced at Ava, but she knew her sister couldn't—or wouldn't—bail her out of this. She fought back the feelings of panic and confusion. She felt like a trapped animal. She knew she had to say something, though.

"I can't go!" Alex blurted out. "I mean, I can go, except not with you."

Corey took a small step back, as though he'd been socked in the abdomen.

"Oh. Okay. Well, see you." He turned to hurry away.

Alex called him back. "Wait! No, it's not like that," she said. "It's only, that, see, um . . ."

Corey waited.

Ava looked up from her phone with an expression that read *Don't say anything dumb!* Too late, though—the words were already tumbling out of Alex's mouth.

"It's just that I have a boyfriend. Back in Massachusetts."

Corey's eyebrows went up.

So did Ava's.

Alex plowed ahead. "His name is . . . um . . ." Alex's eyes flitted wildly around until they came to rest on Ava's phone. "Charlie! His name is Charlie. But, um, I'll still be at Sal's, and I'm sure I'll see you there."

Corey mumbled something Alex couldn't hear and hurried off.

"You have a boyfriend named Charlie? Do I know him?" Ava asked angrily.

"Stop, Ave, I feel bad enough," said Alex. "Ugh! Why do I get so flustered around guys? What is the matter with me? I just felt like I had to have some excuse. Now he hates my guts."

"He doesn't hate your guts."

"Yes, he does."

"Well, at some point you're going to have to come up with a better excuse, because you won't be able to have a boyfriend back home forever."

Alex leaned against the lockers and closed her eyes. "I couldn't think what else to say."

Ava patted her sister on the shoulder. "Come on. Tommy's waiting to talk to us about the anniversary dinner before he goes to practice."

Alex and Ava told their brother the idea for Coach's present to their mom.

"Isn't it an awesome idea?" said Ava.

"Phenomenal," corrected Alex.

"Yeah, that," said Ava.

"Yep, it's phenomenally awesome," said Tommy. He assured them that the music was all set for Thursday. Ava reported that she'd been in touch with Mrs. Cahill about delivering Mrs. Sackett to the restaurant by six thirty.

"So it's all settled," said Alex. "Mom will be so surprised. She thinks it's a ladies' night out."

"Are we going to be there?" asked Ava.

"Having her kids along for her anniversary dinner will thrill Mom to no end," said Tommy.

Alex examined her brother's face. "He's being sarcastic, I think," she said to Ava. "We'll just stay for the very beginning to make sure everything is perfect. And then we'll leave them to a quiet dinner."

"How did you like your new English class?" asked Alex.

The twins were at their lockers the next day, just after sixth period.

"It's so much better," said Ava. "*Johnny Tremain* is the world's most boring book, and I have some catching up to do, obviously, but it's much easier to follow than *White Fang*."

Secretly, she was a little sorry that she and Jack no longer had a single class together. And in spite of all the stress Ms. Palmer's class had caused her, she had to admit to herself that she'd enjoyed the discussions. But she knew things would be better this way. She shoved her English book into her messy locker and rummaged around for her social studies book. One of these days she planned to organize her locker, but she was always running behind and never had the chance.

"How about your class?" she asked Alex, slamming her locker door closed.

Alex bounced up and down, her glossy curls swinging crazily around her shoulders. It was day three of Spirit Week, and everyone was supposed to wear stripes, so Alex had on a new blue-and-white-striped dress that swung around when she moved. It was cut sort of like a cheerleader's dress—and Ava was struck by how natural it looked on Alex.

"Oh, Ave, my new English class is so amazing," she said, pulling a book from her tidy locker shelf and checking her lip gloss in the mirror inside the door. "I do miss Ms. Torres, but she's the debate team coach, so I'll still see her. And I love Ms. Palmer. I've read *White Fang* before, so I'm not behind on that. Today we read some poems by a bunch of different poets, with lines you've heard before like 'Gather ye rosebuds while ye may,' and 'time's winged chariot,' and stuff, and we learned that those are called carpe diem poems."

Ava's eyebrows rose in a question. She loved when her sister was super enthusiastic about something. Her words tended to tumble out of her like coins from a slot machine.

"That means 'seize the day,' and basically that's about enjoying the moment you're in while you're in it, because who knows what will happen tomorrow."

Ava smiled. "That's usually my philosophy—living in the moment—but not necessarily on purpose," she joked. "I'm glad you like your class. And don't look now, but here comes Lindsey."

"Hey, y'all!" said Lindsey brightly. She was wearing black-and-white stripes from head to toe—a matching T-shirt and cropped pants—and orange flats. Even Ava, who thought dressing for Spirit Week was kind of dumb, had to concede she looked stunning.

"So, Alex! What's this I hear about a certain guy of yours?" Her tone was warm and genuine.

"What?" asked Alex, totally confused.

Ava gave her a subtle elbow jab in the ribs.

"Ow! Oh!" Alex clearly remembered, and tried to recover. "Oh, yeah." She feigned a giggle. "Yeah, good old Charlie."

"Can't wait to hear about him!" said Lindsey.

The bell rang, and Lindsey skipped off down the hallway.

"Be sure you come sit with us at the game Friday, okay?" she said over her shoulder.

"Fabulous!" squeaked Alex.

CHAPTER THIRTEEN

Disaster struck Thursday afternoon, a hot and sultry day, as the twins were walking toward Le Pain to make the final preparations for the surprise anniversary dinner. Alex carried a small bouquet of daisies, which were Mrs. Sackett's favorite. They'd looked everywhere around their neighborhood for them without success, and so Alex had had the idea to special order them from an actual florist's shop. She'd picked them up after school the day before and had carefully kept them in water inside her locker. Now in the afternoon heat they were already looking a little droopy.

Ava carried the present their dad was going to give to their mom. It was wrapped in a little box with a purple ribbon. They had arranged to bring everything to Madame Nicole in advance of the dinner.

"Huh, just got a text from Daddy," said Alex with a frown, glancing at her phone.

"Me too," said Ava, pulling out her own phone.

The girls opened their messages at the same time.

Neither one said anything, although Alex let out a tiny gasp.

Then they looked at each other.

"This cannot be happening," said Alex. She felt hot tears springing to her eyes. Even cool, calm Ava looked distressed.

"How could there be a pep rally tonight?" wailed Alex.

"Well, duh, of course there's a pep rally tonight, now that I think of it," said Ava. "The question is, why didn't Coach or Tommy think of it? I mean, it's been Spirit Week all week long. It makes total sense that there'd be a pep rally tonight, the night before the first game of the season."

"Maybe he won't have to go!" said Alex, but she knew perfectly well she was wrong. Of course the head coach of the team would have to go. He'd probably be expected to make a speech.

They leaned against the side of a brick building, near an antique storefront a few doors away from Le Pain. Alex could feel the heat of the bricks through her shirt.

Ava snapped out of it first. She tapped at her phone.

"Who are you calling?" asked Alex, sniffling.

"Coach."

"Daddy? He has practice!"

"Not for three more minutes," she said grimly, and held the phone to her ear. "And he just sent that text, so he'll still have his phone in his hand."

Alex swallowed back a huge lump that had risen in her throat.

"Coach," said Ava, and her tone was businesslike, not accusatory. "We just got your text." (Pause.) "I know." (Pause.) "I know. It's fine." (Pause.) "I know." (Pause.) "I know." (Much longer pause.)

Alex hopped from one foot to the other, wishing she'd thought to get Ava to put him on speakerphone.

"Okay, but we have a plan," said Ava.

"We do?" whispered Alex.

"Yes, we do," said Ava into the phone, because Coach must have asked the same question. "We're almost at the restaurant. We're going to tell Madame Nicole to move the reservation to six fifteen, and we'll have them make the food ahead, so it will be waiting for you when you get here. You hustle from practice just as it ends, at six. The pep rally is at seven. That should give you forty-five minutes for dinner." She paused again while he spoke. "Yes." (Pause.) "Yes." (Pause.) "Yes. I know. We are the best. No one is better than we are. Yup. Bye."

She hung up.

"Well?" Alex asked anxiously.

"I think we're going to be okay," said Ava. "You go to the restaurant and preorder the food and talk to them about the schedule change. Madame Nicole told us she wouldn't accept any other reservations or walk-ins before seven p.m., so they could have the restaurant all to themselves, and this won't change that. It'll just be a faster dinner."

"A much faster dinner," said Alex glumly.

Ava continued, all business. "I'll text Mrs. Cahill and tell her to get Mom there fifteen minutes earlier. Then I'll run over to the stadium and find Coach Byron. I'll ask him to have Coach out of there as early as humanly possible after practice ends. And then I'll track down Tommy and tell him to call the musician and ask him or her to be there fifteen minutes earlier. They'll have forty-five minutes to celebrate their anniversary before he has to go to the pep rally. It's not ideal, but it'll be better than nothing."

Alex took a step back and regarded her sister with newfound admiration. "Ave! You're so organized. You sound like me! Only much more efficient! What's gotten into you?"

Ava grinned and shrugged. "I think now that I know my disorganization and lack of focus have a name, and that I can do something about them, I actually feel better. More organized and focused. Go figure."

"I'm glad for you," Alex said. "But I'm worried about how Mom is going to respond. Did you see how quiet she was at breakfast this morning? She didn't even mention their anniversary. I bet she's convinced Daddy has forgotten it. She was probably waiting for him to wish her a happy anniversary, and he didn't. I hope this isn't going to end in tragedy."

"Me too," said Ava grimly. "Now let's get going. We have a job to do."

Coach walked into the restaurant at 6:01, frazzled and anxious. But his dripping hair told Alex he'd showered, and he'd even managed to put on a collared shirt and dress pants. Alex could hardly believe it.

"Daddy!" she exclaimed, pulling him toward the table. "How did you get out of practice so early? I thought it ended at six!"

Coach shot Ava a look. "Coach Byron booted me at five forty-five," he said. "Told me he'd handle the end of practice and the team talk. He practically slammed the locker room door in my face."

Ava looked up at the ceiling and whistled innocently.

"Well, you look awesome," said Alex. "I mean, dapper."

Coach and Ava looked at each other and laughed.

"It's a shame Tommy can't be here to witness the surprise," said Alex.

"I agree," said Coach. "But the whole team is expected to shower and head straight to the pep rally—I can't do anything about that. Your mother will understand."

"She's going to be here any minute," said Ava, glancing at the clock on her phone.

Coach admired the table. The daisies were arranged in a low cut-crystal vase. Golden light from the votive candles made the silver sparkle and the china glint. He spied Madame Nicole hovering in the background and gave her a thumbs-up. She beamed.

Suddenly he turned toward the girls in a panic.

"A present," he croaked. "I forgot to get her a present."

Alex held out the box with the purple ribbon. "We're all over that, Daddy," she said, and giggled.

"What did I get her?"

"Your varsity ring," she said. "Ava and Tommy and I chipped in and got a silver chain for it so Mom could wear it around her neck, as if you guys were in high school."

"It was Alex's idea," said Ava gallantly.

He marveled at her. "It's perfect, sweetie.

She'll love it." He looked around. "Why are there no other people in the restaurant?"

Madame Nicole stepped out from behind the antique polished bar. "Good evening, Monsieur Sackett," she said.

Alex loved the way she'd pronounced it: *Sah-KET*.

"We were actually planning to be closed tonight," she explained. "We have found that 'istorically, we have very little business on the nights before 'ome football games. And of course tomorrow night we will be open quite late, after ze game, for those who desire a late-night supper."

"That's mighty kind of you, Madame Nicole," said Coach. "I'm sorry about all the confusion with the pep rally. You and my daughters have certainly saved the day!"

"She's here!" yelled Ava from the window, where she'd set up surveillance.

Madame Nicole hurried to the door and pulled it open.

Mrs. Cahill entered first, leading a blindfolded Mrs. Sackett.

Mrs. Sackett was giggling. "This is rather elaborate, April. Where on earth are we going?"

Mrs. Cahill didn't answer, but led Mrs. Sackett over to the table, where Coach had leaped up to pull out her chair. Then he untied the blindfold.

Mrs. Sackett blinked and looked around, a bewildered expression on her face. "Michael! Alex? Ava? What on earth—," she said. "I thought we were having a girls' night!"

"Happy anniversary!" yelled Ava and Alex at the same time.

Mrs. Sackett's eyes widened. She clapped both her hands to her mouth.

Ava bent over in silent laughter. Then she stood and whispered into Alex's ear. "She totally forgot it was their anniversary! She's as bad as Coach!"

Mrs. Cahill congratulated them, gave Mrs. Sackett a quick hug, patted Coach on the shoulder, and left the restaurant.

Coach helped their mom sit and gently pushed in her chair. "It was these girls of ours who arranged everything," he said. "They planned this whole thing. We have the whole restaurant to ourselves. Can you imagine? A quiet dinner, just the two of us?"

Just then, music started playing.

Ava and Alex looked up, startled. It was live

music, but not a violin; it was lovely, sassy, jazzy music.

Madame Nicole wheeled away an accordion divider that had been obscuring part of the room near their parents' table, and which Alex hadn't even noticed hadn't been there the last time they visited the restaurant.

Behind it were Tommy and two of his friends. Tommy was still in his practice pads, his cheeks flushed with recent exertion and with traces of eye black still on his face, but he was sitting at a piano, playing as though he were wearing a snappy tuxedo. Next to him, a handsome high school boy tapped rhythmically on a drum set, and a girl in a sleek blue dress and shiny silver heels plucked away at a double bass.

Tommy glanced up at them and gave them a half smile without missing a beat.

The other four Sacketts gaped in astonishment.

"Aha, you see?" said Madame Nicole. "Even I can 'elp with the surprises!"

Mrs. Sackett dabbed away a tear from the corner of her eye with her table napkin. "Oh, Michael. Girls. It's perfect. It's just so lovely."

"Yeah, about that," said Coach, shifting uncomfortably in his chair and darting a glance toward the kitchen. "I'm afraid we don't have all the time in the world for dinner." He glanced at his watch. "But at least we have, uh, thirty-two minutes together."

"Pep rally?" asked Mrs. Sackett.

"Yes," he said, nodding apologetically. "Which of course you know all about, because you probably helped plan it."

Mrs. Sackett nodded, and reached across the table to clasp his hands in hers. "It's okay, honey," she said. "Just the fact that you pulled this off is a miracle in itself."

Ava whispered into Alex's ear. "It's turning goopy," she said.

"Right," said Alex quickly. "I think we should get going."

"Yeah, we'll leave you two alone," said Ava.

"For your quiet, romantic half hour together," added Alex.

"Do you hear a noise?" asked Mrs. Sackett.

The door to the restaurant burst open.

CHAPTER FOURTEEN

A mob of people streamed into the restaurant. Just behind them was a large portion of the Ashland High School marching band. Tommy's trio stopped playing and settled back to watch, grinning. Ava stared at her brother. Was he in on this?

The band was playing the school song. In the small room, the noise was almost deafening. A gleaming sousaphone loomed above the crowd of heads, as well as a tuba and at least one trombone. Bringing up the rear was a blond-haired high school boy booming on the big bass drum. Ava was pretty sure she could see dishes vibrating.

Six or seven cheerleaders in uniform were punching the air with pom-poms. Ava wondered if the pretty girl in the middle of the group with her hair braided was Kylie's older sister. She suspected so. Then, when Ava was sure the restaurant couldn't hold any more people, the crowd parted to make way for at least a dozen members of the football team and all the assistant coaches. Everyone cheered and whooped over the sound of the band.

Now the tiny restaurant was packed wall-to-wall. Ava found herself backed up against the front window, and she could see that outside, hundreds—could it be thousands?—of townspeople were gathered, singing, cheering, chanting, in the golden light of the setting sun.

Madame Nicole stood up on a chair, the way ladies in cartoons did when they saw a mouse. But rather than looking alarmed, she was smiling and conducting the band, her elegant, bracelet-adorned arms making half circles in the air with an invisible baton. Ava wondered if she had known about this new plan, and suspected that she had. Most likely Tommy had tipped her off.

She could see the kitchen staff, who had all come out into the dining area to observe the action. No wonder the *amuse-bouche*—which Alex had found out was kind of a single-serving appetizer—hadn't been brought out yet!

When the band finished the school song, Coach Byron gave a quick toot on his whistle to quiet the crowd. He, too, stood up on a chair. Ava could see his two kids, Jamila and Shane, hovering near Mr. and Mrs. Sackett's table.

"Laura," said Coach Byron, nodding toward Mrs. Sackett. "Coach Sackett, members of the team, members of the pep squad, PTA organizers, townspeople, and random passersby who just wandered in to see what the fuss was about"—everyone laughed—"welcome! We've gathered here to wish Laura and Coach Sackett a happy anniversary. I understand from Tom that it's your twentieth." He gave Tommy a little salute.

Tommy saluted back.

"And we've also learned over these past couple of weeks that Coach is somewhat stubborn and that the last thing in the world he'd consider is missing tonight's pep rally, even if it is his twentieth wedding anniversary."

Lots of people in the crowd laughed again. One of the horn players tooted playfully.

"And so," continued Coach Byron, "we decided that rather than have you come to the pep rally, we'd bring it to you, Coach. So here we are!"

Another big cheer. Honking horns. Waving pom-poms.

"A big thanks to your daughters, Ava and Alex, for organizing this intimate romantic dinner for you," he said.

The crowd laughed again.

"And to Madame Nicole Duchamps and her husband, Gaston, the co-owners of this quiet little romantic restaurant."

The chef—Ava assumed Monsieur Gaston—acknowledged the crowd with a wave of his whisk. Madame Nicole had borrowed an air horn from one of the boys in the crowd, and she gave it a blaring toot, eliciting another howl of laughter from the crowd.

Coach stood up from his chair and cleared his throat, but Coach Byron put up his hands to prevent him from speaking.

"No speeches, Coach!"

More laughter.

"We aren't here to ask you to make an on-demand speech on your anniversary. We just came by to wish you well, to extend our apologies to Laura for taking you away from your family for so many hours of the day so many days of the week, and to tell you we're heading off to the stadium for the pep rally, and we want you to stay here and enjoy your dinner. And to extend a special, heartfelt thanks to Laura, for all the great work she's done for the team so far."

Several parents in the back of the crowd whooped loudly at that.

Mrs. Sackett beamed.

"Go, Tigers!" shouted Coach Byron.

With a roar and a cheer that made Ava fear for the windowpanes in the restaurant, the crowd began filing out. The band started up the school song again, and in a few minutes the room was quiet, although they could hear the shouts and cheers and music and horn blares as they receded into the distance.

Tommy and his musician friends stopped by the table. The two friends shook hands with Coach and Mrs. Sackett and headed off, leaving Tommy, Alex, and Ava alone with their parents.

Mrs. Sackett shook her head in wonderment. "You kids. Michael. I just, I don't know what to say." She sniffled, her eyes misty.

"Make her open the present, Daddy!" said Alex excitedly.

Coach grinned as Mrs. Sackett pulled the lid off the little box and exclaimed in delight at the class ring on a chain. Alex helped her fasten it. They all admired how pretty it looked.

Then Mrs. Sackett looked guiltily at Coach.

"Michael, I am the worst wife ever," she said. "I completely forgot about our anniversary. It's been so hectic this week I just—it slipped my mind. And here you did all this planning."

Coach shifted uncomfortably in his chair, darted a sideways look at Ava and Alex, cleared his throat, and said, "To be honest, Laur, it was Alex who remembered. And she and Ave and Tommy did all the planning. I would have forgotten too. So don't beat yourself up about it. We've both been a little—distracted. The difference is, I'm so bad, the kids knew I'd forget. At least they gave you more credit, and rightfully so."

Mrs. Sackett put her arm around Alex's waist and pulled her daughter close to her. "I am the luckiest person on the planet," she said, "to have such an amazing family."

"We wanted you to know how much we appreciate all that you do, Mom," said Alex.

Ava and Tommy nodded.

"Come on, dudes," said Tommy to his sisters. "Let's head to the rally and leave these two love-birds to their romantic dinner."

Later that night Ava lay in bed, flush with happiness about the success of the dinner and the fun she'd had at the pep rally. She'd stood next to Jack the whole time.

Her phone buzzed. It was Charlie, from back home.

What's up, cowboy? All good?

Yeah, great. Big pep rally tonight.

Another text came in, but this one was from Jack. Jack! She was getting near-simultaneous texts from two different guys!

Hey—it was so noisy at the rally. Barely had a chance to talk to you. I heard your parents' surprise dinner was awesome.

She texted him back, after triple-checking that it was going to Jack, not Charlie.

Yeah, it worked out really well!

From Charlie: Your dad's team supposed to win tomorrow?

From Jack: I'll look for you at the game tomorrow.

> **To Charlie:** I think it's going to be a tough game.

From Jack: Will you be at Sal's after?

> **To Jack:** Yeah, I think so.

She fell back on the pillow. Texting two boys at the same time. That was definitely a first.

Meanwhile, Alex was in her room, picking her outfit for the next day—game day, and the last day of Spirit Week, and everyone was supposed to wear Tigers stuff. She'd borrowed a practice jersey from Tommy, which she planned to knot at the waist over her new pair of skinny blue capris.

She replayed the events of the evening in her

head. The restaurant episode had been—what was a good word? Sensational. That was it. And the pep rally had been exhilarating.

Their parents had arrived home just a few minutes after she and Tommy and Ava had. They'd had a long, luxurious, quiet dinner, they said, and the food was amazing. Madame Nicole had had a special dessert prepared for them, and they'd brought the rest of it home for the kids. It was a heart-shaped chocolate cake, coated in a glossy chocolate shell, beneath which was a rich chocolate buttercream. It was the best cake Alex had ever tasted.

Her mind moved to Corey. Was he furious with her because she'd said she had a boyfriend? Was that all it had taken to get Lindsey to be genuinely nice to her? Was it worth it?

Her homework done, she pulled out the book she'd borrowed from the library: *Tackling the Game of Football*. She really needed to learn more about how football was played so she stopped sounding like a total dope when asked about her dad's team. But five minutes into reading about types of offense, her eyes began to droop, and she turned out the light and fell asleep.

CHAPTER FIFTEEN

"Mom, no offense, but I hope you understand that we can't possibly be seen sitting with you," Alex shouted over the din. She, Ava, and their mother made their way through the crowds standing along the sidelines and headed toward the midfield bleachers. The band was playing and the crowd was already assembling, even though it was still a while until kickoff.

"Of course," Mrs. Sackett yelled back. "I understand that being seen with your mother is a fate worse than death in middle school. In fact, why don't you girls drop back a bit so we're not seen walking together? As soon as I can find April, I'll make myself scarce, I promise."

Alex looked quickly at her mother's face to

be sure she wasn't upset. She didn't seem to be. She had a—what was that word she'd studied?—implacable, that was it. She had an implacable smile on her face.

"Okay, thanks, Mom," said Alex.

Ava had already dropped back, having understood their mother's joking tone more quickly.

"There's April," yelled Mrs. Sackett over her shoulder. "Just wish me luck. The entire Ashland PTA is standing all around her."

"Good luck," the twins called to her at the same time.

They stood back and watched as sure enough, Mrs. Sackett was enveloped in a crowd of other moms and dads and was carried into the current of people streaming toward the higher decks.

Darkness had not yet settled in, and the lights had not yet been illuminated. The sun was low in the sky, and a golden glow flooded through the stadium. Alex had read somewhere that photographers and painters called this the golden hour, the first and last hour of sunlight during the day when the light was perfect for creating beautiful images. She looked at her twin sister, who was bathed in golden light. It picked up the coppery tones of her dark hair and cast a rosy sheen on her skin. Both girls had their mother's fair, smooth complexion.

"I can't believe how crowded it is already," shouted Ava.

Alex gaped at the crowds. "I thought we'd be the only ones here this early," she shouted back. "I was so worried we'd sit in empty stands and then all the popular kids would sit somewhere else. But I think I see Lindsey and Emily up there already!"

"You go on ahead," said Ava. "I just spotted Kylie sitting by herself with a book. She probably had to get here early with her older sister. I'll go keep her company."

Alex smiled. "Okay, if you're sure." She made her way up into the stands to where Lindsey, Emily, and several other girls she knew were sitting.

As soon as Lindsey spotted Alex, she made a big show of clearing a space between her and Rosa to make room for Alex to sit down.

"I'm so psyched for the first game!" she said. "Is your dad totally freaking out?"

"Surprisingly, he's kept pretty cool," replied Alex, taken aback by Lindsey's intensely enthusiastic attitude toward her. *So I was right,* she thought. *She was only being mean to me because of Corey, and now that she thinks I have a boyfriend, she's being friendly.* The relief that washed over Alex as she realized she was finally on track with the popular crowd didn't entirely eliminate the sad, guilty feeling she kept getting in her stomach when she thought about the look on Corey's face after she'd told him about Charlie.

"Sooooo," said Emily, drawing the word out in a playful, teasing tone. She sat on Lindsey's other side and leaned in conspiratorially so the three of them were practically in a huddle. "Tell us more about Charlie! Is he totally cute? What does he look like? Does he play football? Does your daddy approve of him?"

Alex slumped. Should she continue to play along with this story, or back down and admit she'd made it up? The latter plan didn't seem like a good one. Corey seemed hurt enough that she'd rejected him; he'd probably never speak to her again if he found out she'd lied about that.

"Oh, ha," she said, laughing mirthlessly. "Yeah, he's pretty good-looking. He's tall, with reddish hair." *Ugh, this is so weird, describing Ava's crush,* she thought. She tried desperately to think of a way to change the subject, but

Lindsey and Emily seemed to be hanging on her every word, wanting more. "We—uh, we haven't been texting too much recently, with all the craziness that's been going on this week with my parents' anniversary and the first game and all."

She hated lying. She never lied. Her stomach was starting to feel queasy.

"Oh yes, the anniversary dinner for your parents," said Lindsey. "That's so romantic. I couldn't believe what happened last night with the pep rally. I wish I could have been there, but they had to limit the numbers and only allowed the seniors into the restaurant."

"Although we were outside," added Emily. "A whole bunch of your friends were there!"

Alex beamed. To think that so many of the popular middle school kids had bothered to come to the restaurant like that! Talk about great free publicity for her class president campaign. Plus, she felt so relieved that the conversation had moved away from her imaginary boyfriend.

"You're good at organizing big events," said Lindsey. "Em and I were just talking about you. She told me you were thinking of running for class president. I think you'd be great—better than Logan Medina, who wins every year just 'cause he's a popular jock."

Emily nodded vigorously, her blond ponytail swaying.

"Wow, thanks, you guys," said Alex breathlessly. "I'm glad you think it's a good idea." *Maybe giving up Corey and lying about Charlie will be worth it after all,* she thought.

"What about Ava?" asked Emily. "Is she as good at organizing events as you are? Maybe she should be in government too."

Alex laughed. "Student government is not her thing. She's a jock, just like our brother."

"So is she going out for cross-country?" asked Emily.

Alex hesitated. How would these girls react when they found out Ava was trying out for football? She decided to come right out with it and see if she could gauge their reactions.

"She signed up for football," said Alex.

Emily and Lindsey both laughed but grew serious when they saw Alex's straight face.

Alex cringed. This plan of Ava's was not going to go over well at their new school. Girls didn't play football here. The last thing Alex wanted, for her or for Ava, was to cause a stir just as they were riding the tide of the anniversary dinner and pep rally and finally settling into life at this new school. Maybe she could talk Ava out of it. For now, she decided to change the subject.

"Are you going to this Sal's place after the game?" she asked Emily.

"Of course!" said Emily. "Everyone will be there. And they have pretty good pizza, too."

"Good. I hope it's better than the restaurant my dad took us to last week. I think it was called Eli's or something. Bleh." Alex made a face. "Everything had meat in it."

The girls didn't respond. Lindsey seemed suddenly to be engrossed in a text.

Alex felt a stab of horror. *Wait. Oh, no. Is it possible that Eli's is Lindsey's family's restaurant?* She'd never actually asked what it was called. From the way Lindsey was behaving, and how quiet Emily had grown, it was probably Eli's.

Just when she was getting somewhere with these girls, she'd sabotaged herself. At this rate, Ava could join the football team and the wrestling squad and Alex would still be the one to make everyone dislike them.

"Two minutes till kickoff, Kylie," said Ava as she walked up to her friend. "I forbid you to read a book once the game has started."

Kylie closed her book immediately and grinned at Ava. "Hey, you!" she said. "I'm so honored to be sitting with Coach Sackett's daughter at the big game. Shouldn't you be sitting with your public?"

"Please," said Ava. "I don't want to sit with all those kids up there. I doubt they even watch the game. They're probably too busy gossiping. I'm not even sure *Alex* watches the game. She barely knows the difference between a quarterback and a running back."

"Is there a difference?"

Ava playfully punched Kylie in the arm. "Funny. Anyway, that's why I'm sitting with you. So I can concentrate on the game."

"Well, trust me. I won't bother you," said Kylie. "Considering I don't know a quarterback from a running back from my big toe."

"I'll explain what's going on during the game," said Ava.

"Okay. I'm willing to be converted."

The noise of the crowd swelled.

"It's kickoff time!" yelled Ava.

CHAPTER SIXTEEN

"Who's Dion?" demanded Kylie, looking up from her phone.

Ava turned. "He's the backup quarterback to PJ Kelly," she explained. "Why?"

"I just got a text from my sister," said Kylie. "She says that Dion is out. He has a stress fracture."

Ava's eyes widened.

"Is that big news?" asked Kylie.

"Well, yeah," Ava said. "Because with Dion out, that makes my brother, Tom, the backup quarterback, just behind PJ."

"Oh! That's pretty cool," said Kylie.

Ava's stomach flipped over. Of course it was highly unlikely Tommy would get into the game, but it could happen. She wondered what was going through her brother's mind.

"Chances are he won't actually get to play. Tommy's only a sophomore," she said to Kylie. "And PJ is really good."

"Hey, you never know," said Kylie. "Where's your dad?"

Ava pointed. "He's there, on the sideline. He's the one with the big headphones on. That way he can communicate with the assistant coaches up there in the tower."

Kylie looked behind them to where Ava was pointing. She whistled. "Wow. I always wondered who those people up there were."

"They're coaches, and also video people and TV camera guys," Ava explained. She smiled at her new friend. Kylie seemed genuinely interested in paying attention to the game.

The Mainville Eagles won the toss, so they started with the ball. But Ashland's defense stopped the first drive. Then, just at the three-minute mark, the Ashland Tigers scored a touchdown. The crowd went wild.

"Yaaaaay!" yelled Kylie along with everyone else. "That's good, right?"

"That's good, but it's early," said Ava. She

glanced down at her dad, who was yelling something into the mouthpiece of his headphones and
pacing up and down along the sidelines. He was
looking at PJ in disbelief. Ava wondered why.

And sure enough, Mainville scored two unan-
swered touchdowns and led for the rest of the
half, fourteen to seven.

During the halftime show Kylie went off to the
refreshment stand. Ava was too nervous to do
anything but sit and pretend to be watching
the high-steppers and the band, although her
mind was a million miles away, thinking about
the game, about Tommy, and about her dad. It
would be so awful if he lost his first game. She
hoped no one would come try to talk to her.
Thankfully, they didn't, and the game resumed.

"What's going on?" yelled Kylie at the end of
the third quarter. The Ashland fans were booing.

Ava turned to explain. "We were in a good
position to score. We had that interception, and
our safety made a really good return to set up a
touchdown. But PJ is not having a good game.
He just had three incomplete passes, and that

fourth-down running play got snuffed. So now it's Mainville's ball."

The Ashland Tigers managed to stop the Mainville team from scoring. Then the offensive squad trotted onto the field. The Ashland fans booed even louder.

"What? What's happening?" demanded Kylie.

Ava's jaw fell open. "It looks like Coach has yanked PJ," she said to Kylie. "Tommy's in."

Something isn't right, she thought. A coach didn't usually pull out the first-string quarterback—an experienced senior—in the middle of the first game of the season, unless the quarterback was injured, and Ava hadn't seen PJ get hurt. The other reason might be that the coach wanted to teach him a lesson. She remembered what Tommy had said, about PJ being all over the place. Maybe he'd done something to really make Coach mad.

The score remained the same. Ava could sense the Ashland fans' unease. Maybe they were blaming Coach for the way the game was going. He had so much to prove to everyone.

And then, in the fourth quarter, Tommy completed a pass to Tyler Whitley in the end zone with four minutes and twenty-two seconds left.

The score was fourteen to thriteen. The crowd rose to its feet, roaring.

"Woooo!" yelled Kylie, jumping up and down. "We scored! We're going to win!"

Ava cheered too, but she'd learned not to let down her guard. Ashland had an uphill battle ahead if they were going to beat this team.

A few minutes later it was the Mainville fans' turn to roar.

Ava groaned as the Mainville band played a triumphant tune and the other team's fans all stomped and clapped along.

"What! What just happened?" asked Kylie. "Why did that guy just get to run all that way? Why didn't we tackle him?"

"Mainville had a sixty-one-yard kickoff return," said Ava. "We should have stopped their guy, but we didn't. And now—" She groaned again, as did the rest of the Tigers fans.

"Touchdown?" asked Kylie softly.

Ava nodded. She put up a finger to indicate that Kylie should wait.

The Tigers fans erupted in cheers.

"We just blocked the extra point. So the score is twenty to thirteen."

The girls watched the scoreboard click

through a blur of numbers until it read HOME: 13, OPPONENT: 20.

"Can we get a touchdown in one minute, forty seconds?" asked Kylie anxiously.

In spite of Ava's anguish, she was pleased to note how into the game Kylie was.

"It's going to be close," said Ava.

"Now what's happening?" demanded Kylie.

"It's the second down and—wait—oh, Tommy come on, come on—"

Ava's voice was drowned out in the roar of the crowd. Many of the Tigers fans reached out their hands to grasp an imaginary football, as though collectively willing the long pass Tommy had thrown to be caught by Tyler.

Tyler caught the pass at his own thirty-yard line and intentionally ran out of bounds.

"Why did he do that?" demanded Kylie. "So those two goons wouldn't tackle him?"

"To stop the clock," said Ava. "He knew they were about to tackle him, and if they'd done so on the field, the clock would have run down. When he runs out of bounds, the clock stops."

Kylie nodded, trying to chew on eight of her fingernails at the same time.

"I'm going to sit down," she shouted to Ava

over the roaring fans. "My nerves can't stand it. Can you poke me when something big happens?"

"Okay, now you have to stand up," yelled Ava a few minutes later.

Kylie stood up. "All right—tell me."

"It's fourth down with eight yards to go at the thirty-eight-yard line. We have one chance to get a touchdown, and the other team knows Tommy's going to pass it, because there's no time for a running play. Because look how much time is on the clock."

Kylie gulped. "Seven seconds!" she croaked.

Tommy threw the pass high. A perfect spiral.

The crowd on both sides went almost silent as the pass was in the air. The whole stadium seemed to be holding its breath.

Ava felt Kylie's fingers dig into her arm.

Then the crowd went crazy.

"He caught it!" screamed Kylie, but no one noticed, because everyone else in the Tigers stands was screaming too, including Ava.

Kylie stopped jumping up and down. "But wait! The score is only twenty to nineteen, and there's no time on the clock. Why is everyone still screaming? Did we lose or didn't we?"

"We get to attempt the extra point," said Ava. "The question is, are we going to kick for the extra point to tie, or are we going for two?"

"I certainly don't know," said Kylie. "I'm going to sit down and put my head between my knees."

Many people around them groaned.

"Did we lose?" asked Kylie, lifting her head back up.

"No. They're worried because we're going for two points. They think it's risky and we should take the tie."

Time seemed to stand still again. Once more, the huge stadium got quiet.

Ava watched Tommy take the snap and fake a handoff to the running back. And then—

"It's a bootleg!" screamed Ava. "Tommy's running!"

Kylie jumped to her feet.

Ava gasped. "He's down—"

Tommy was buried under a mound of defense at the goal line.

Ava realized she hadn't breathed in quite some time.

There was utter silence in the stadium for what felt like the longest second of Ava's life.

Then the Ashland fans went crazy as the referee in the end zone raised both arms straight above his head.

Tommy had scored. The scoreboard clicked to twenty-one to twenty. The Tigers had won.

After the game the crowd swarmed the field. Tommy was carried off on the other players' shoulders. Coach was doused with the ice-water bucket. Ava was as delirious as everyone else, dancing with Kylie, hugging Alex, hugging her mom. Jack came running up to her and gave her a double high five. Even Ms. Palmer, the English teacher, gave the girls a big hug. It was a little weird being hugged by a teacher, Ava thought, especially one in whose class you'd flunked two quizzes. But she went with it.

"Don't forget that we're all going to Sal's for pizza!" Alex yelled into Ava's ear. "But not right away. I'll text you when we're all heading over!"

Ava gave her a thumbs-up. It was too noisy to have a real conversation, and she couldn't really put into words what she was feeling anyway, but she knew her twin felt it too. It was exhilaration, relief, and something else, something neither probably knew how to explain. Ava wondered if it was a little bit of fear. The fear that this evening was short-lived, that every Friday night this season would be a new and fretful experience, and that like it or not, the two of them were going to be in the spotlight.

Kylie promised to show up at Sal's with only a little persuasion, and then went to find her sister.

Ava's throat had gone hoarse from all the cheering. She went in search of a drinking fountain. She was wandering in a semiquiet corridor of the stadium when she felt her phone vibrate. Her eyes widened. It was Tommy!

She hurried to a place in the corridor where the wall jutted out, squeezed herself into the corner, and answered.

"Tommy! Hey!"

"Hey yourself, dude. Pretty cool, huh?" It was extremely noisy in the background where Tommy was. Ava had to strain to be able to make out what he was saying. He was probably calling her from the locker room.

"Tom, that was an unbelievable game," said Ava.

"Yeah, I know," he said. "But things are a little messed up with the team. Hold on. I need to go into the trainer's office a second where they won't hear me."

She heard the noise fade somewhat and a door close.

"That better?"

"Much. So what happened? What's going on with the team?"

"I'll tell you, Ave, but you can't go running to tell all your friends. This isn't something we want circulating on Ashland Middle School's social networks."

"Duh, of course not," said Ava, feeling slightly hurt. Tommy knew perfectly well that she was not a gossip.

"Not even Alex, okay? She's my sister and all, but I wouldn't be surprised if she put it into one of her campaign commercials."

"Okay!" said Ava. Her curiosity was overwhelming. "Tell me what happened!"

"Coach is super mad at PJ," said Tommy. "All game long he was running audibles at the line."

"What are those again?"

"It's when the coach signals a play and then the QB calls a different play when he sees how the defense is lining up. It's totally okay to do once in a while. But PJ did it the whole game. He kept running a different play from the one Coach wanted him to run. Like he didn't trust him or something, like he thought he knew better than Coach. And then during that final drive, he totally ignored Coach's signal to pass, and ran his own running play. So Coach finally yanked him."

"Oh wow," said Ava.

"Yeah, so it's great we won and all, but we've got some team stuff to work through."

"Well, I'm really proud of you, Tom," said Ava.

"Thanks," said Tommy. "I'm enjoying the moment, but I don't know if I'm cut out for this kind of stardom."

"I understand," said Ava, and she did. She knew Tommy's heart was more in his music than football. "But enjoy the moment tonight, okay? Seize the day, as Alex has started saying. She learned about it in her English class for geniuses."

He promised he would. As soon as the call ended, Ava got a text from Alex saying it was time for the pizza party.

CHAPTER SEVENTEEN

Alex and Ava stood outside Sal's.

"I think the gang is already in there," said Alex. "But it's just as well that we got here a little late. We can make an entrance."

"I don't especially want to make an entrance," protested Ava. "And I told Kylie she had to come even though she said she didn't want to. What if she's in there and has no one to talk to?"

"She'll be fine," Alex assured her. "I think this is our moment, Ave. I mean, no matter what people really think of us—like Lindsey, who, by the way, I've managed to upset again—winning that game makes it all just fine, at least for one night. And not only is our dad the coach, but our brother was the star! Did you see him, Ave?"

Ava laughed. "Yep, I saw him, Al. I was there too. He was awesome."

"You know what? I kind of, sort of get what you see in football. I was totally into the game. I've been reading up on the rules, and from now on I'm going to pay attention when you and Daddy and Tommy talk about the game."

Ava smiled at her sister. "Thanks, Alex. I'm kind of, sort of starting to see your point about planning ahead. I've been trying to do stuff ahead of time and not wait till the last minute. And now that I'm in the right English class, I even like what we're studying. It's a strange feeling."

"Good, but let's not think about all that stuff now," said Alex. "Tonight we're going to be celebrities, whether we want to be or not. Personally, I'm looking forward to it. Come on. Let's go in." Alex linked arms with her sister and took a breath, and in they went.

The restaurant was crowded with kids, mostly middle schoolers. Alex immediately spied Emily, Lindsey, Corey, Jack, and even Ava's friend Kylie, who was chattering away with a group of girls.

Suddenly a cheer rose up. Everyone had spotted the twins standing in the doorway.

A man in an apron ran over to greet them, and Alex deduced that he must be Sal. By this time Alex had stopped asking how people knew who she and her sister were. She was used to people in the town just knowing. Sal gathered the two alarmed girls into a huge bear hug. As soon as he'd released them, they were clapped on the back by so many people, so enthusiastically, that Alex had to suppress a small coughing fit.

"Free Cokes all around!" shouted Sal exuberantly, and an even louder cheer went up around the restaurant.

"Over here! Over here, Alex!" shouted Emily.

Alex waved back happily, glanced toward Ava, who nodded back to say *sure, go ahead,* and headed over to the group. As she sat down in a chair that had been hastily vacated for her, she saw Ava sit down next to Kylie.

The waiters and waitresses were busily weaving through the tables with laden trays, doling out the free sodas. Alex was swarmed with well-wishers, congratulating her on her brother's amazing game. Through a gap in the crowd, she and Ava caught each other's eye across the restaurant in a look of happiness and giddiness tinged with a bit of apprehension. From across the restaurant, Alex raised her soda in a little toast and mouthed the words, "Seize the day!"

Just as Ava did exactly the same thing.

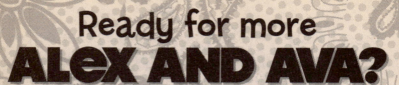

Ready for more
ALEX AND AVA?

**Here's a sneak peek at the next book
in the It Takes Two series:**

Double or
Nothing

"Alex?"

No answer.

"Alex?"

Not so much as a twitch. Ava took a step into
the room. The shades were up, but it was still
dim and shadowy in her sister's bedroom, as the
September sun had not yet risen.

"Al!"

Alex, a gray lump beneath the gray covers,
mumbled something Ava couldn't hear and
turned her back to her sister.

Desperate times called for desperate mea-
sures. Ava strode in and sat down heavily on her
twin's bed, causing the lump under the covers to
give a little bounce. Then she pulled the pillow

out from under her sleeping sister's head.

Alex sat up, her long, curly hair wild, her hands groping blindly. "What? What! Time to get up! What day is it?" A second later, her eyes focused on Ava. Her expression turned from sleepy confusion to wide-awake panic. "Ava!" she whispered, throwing back the covers. "Did I oversleep?"

Ava stood up. She was glad Alex wasn't sick or anything, but this was still weird: Alex never overslept. She was always the first one up; annoyingly chipper in the morning, to the dismay of Ava, who was not a morning person, and their older brother, Tommy, who wasn't a morning person either.

"Yes, but you're not going to be late," said Ava. "We have plenty of time before the bus comes."

"Plenty of time!" repeated Alex as she flew to her chair and grabbed the clothes she'd laid out the night before. "Twenty minutes is not 'plenty of time.'" She headed toward the bathroom. "How could I have overslept today, of all days! I have seventy-eight signatures, and I still need twenty-two more by the end of the day."

"Relax, Al," said Ava. "Just don't spend

nineteen minutes on your hair today and you'll be fine."

Ava heard her twin grunt and slam the door to the bathroom, which was between their bedrooms. A second later, she heard the shower going.

Ava stood and contemplated her sister's neat-as-a-pin bedroom, now bathed in pinky-gold tones as the sun rose in the eastern sky. Alex's clipboard was on the top of the tidy pile of books on her desk. She was running for seventh-grade class president at Ashland Middle School, and campaign petitions were due today. But today was a big day for both of them; she, Ava, had slept fitfully all night long and finally gotten up before her alarm had rung. This afternoon was the first day of football tryouts, and she was a combination of excited and nervous.

The kitchen was bustling when Ava entered. Coach Sackett had his orange Ashland Tigers hat on, his briefcase was near the door, and he had just finished packing the girls' lunches. Mrs. Sackett was still in her workout clothes— an oversize Patriots T-shirt and yoga pants—her long, curly hair pulled back into a ponytail. She had just come back from walking Moxy, the Sacketts' Australian shepherd. Tommy's mouth was full—a common occurrence—as he downed what remained of his bacon-egg-and-cheese sandwich and stood up from the table.

"Alex overslept," announced Ava.

Coach froze in mid-swig of coffee.

Tommy stopped chewing.

Mrs. Sackett stood, holding Moxy's food dish.

They all gaped at Ava.

"Wow. Alex overslept?" said Tommy.

"Is she feeling sick?" asked Mrs. Sackett. Moxy thumped her tail loudly on the kitchen floor, waiting for Mrs. Sackett to set the bowl down.

"Nope, she's fine," said Ava, pouring out her cereal. "She was probably up late texting with Emily about her campaign strategy."

Coach grabbed his briefcase, pecked Mrs. Sackett good-bye on the cheek, and leaned across the table to ruffle Ava's already-mussed-up hair.

"Hey, careful there, Coach. I worked hard on my hairstyle this morning," said Ava. She twirled a piece of short, curly brown hair around her finger and laughed.

"Good luck at tryouts today, darlin'," he said, heading for the door. "Remember to stay low and move those feet."

Ava grinned. "I will, Coach. I will." Was his

Texas accent re-emerging? He had grown up near Ashland but had lived in the Northeast for most of his adult life. They'd been back in Texas for several weeks now, and Ava was starting to detect an accent creeping back into his voice. Subtle stuff—like dropping the g's on his –ing word endings. She made a mental note to ask Alex if she had noticed this too.

Alex hurried into the kitchen just after Tommy and Coach had backed out of the drive-way and driven away. Her expression was frazzled, but the rest of her looked as smooth and put-together as ever. "Mom, no time for breakfast," she said, picking up her lunch and swinging her backpack onto her shoulder. "I need to get to the bus stop in time to plan my strategy. I need seventh graders to sign my clipboard."

Mrs. Sackett handed Alex a piece of toast and a peeled banana on a paper towel and nodded. She probably knew there was no arguing with Alex about the importance of a good breakfast on a day like today. "Good luck today, girls," she said, as the sisters traipsed to the door, laden down with heavy backpacks. "It's a big day for both of you."

Belle Payton isn't a twin herself, but she does have twin brothers! She spent much of her childhood in the bleachers reading—er, cheering them on—at their football games. Though she left the South long ago to become a children's book editor in New York City, Belle still drinks approximately a gallon of sweet tea a week and loves treating her friends to her famous homemade mac-and-cheese. Belle is the author of many books for children and tweens, and is currently having a blast writing two sides to each It Takes Two story.